THE BUILDING OF THE GREAT PYRAMID

Three Reports from c.2600BC:
A Trilogy of Parables for our Time

JOHN HUNT PUBLISHING

First published by Liberalis Books, 2024
Liberalis Books is an imprint of John Hunt Publishing Ltd., 3 East St., Alresford,
Hampshire SO24 9EE, UK
office@jhpbooks.com
www.johnhuntpublishing.com
www.o-books.com

For distributor details and how to order please visit the 'Ordering' section on our website.

Text copyright: Nicholas Hagger 2021

ISBN: 978 1 78535 159 4
978 1 78535 160 0 (ebook)
Library of Congress Control Number: 2021942239

A CIP catalogue record for this book is available from the British Library.

Design: Stuart Davies

UK: Printed and bound by CPI Group (UK) Ltd, Croydon, CR0 4YY
Printed in North America by CPI GPS partners

We operate a distinctive and ethical publishing philosophy in all areas
of our business, from our global network of authors to production and
worldwide distribution.

THE BUILDING OF THE GREAT PYRAMID

Three Reports from c.2600BC:
A Trilogy of Parables for our Time

Nicholas Hagger

LIBERALIS
BOOKS

Winchester, UK
Washington, USA

Also by Nicholas Hagger

The Fire and the Stones
Selected Poems
The Universe and the Light
A White Radiance
A Mystic Way
Awakening to the Light
A Spade Fresh with Mud
The Warlords
Overlord
A Smell of Leaves and Summer
The Tragedy of Prince Tudor
The One and the Many
Wheeling Bats and a Harvest Moon
The Warm Glow of the Monastery Courtyard
The Syndicate
The Secret History of the West
The Light of Civilization
Classical Odes
Overlord, one-volume edition
Collected Poems 1958–2005
Collected Verse Plays
Collected Stories
The Secret Founding of America
The Last Tourist in Iran
The Rise and Fall of Civilizations
The New Philosophy of Universalism
The Libyan Revolution
Armageddon
The World Government
The Secret American Dream
A New Philosophy of Literature
A View of Epping Forest
My Double Life 1: This Dark Wood

The front cover shows the Great Pyramid at Giza, Egypt.

Acknowledgments

I am grateful to my wife Ann for accompanying me to Egypt in 2005 and 2020; and to my PA Ingrid Kirk for assembling this book during Covid-19 lockdown between 22 March and 30 April 2021, while working on other books remotely from home when face-to-face meetings were impossible. Without her help this book could not have been completed so quickly.

Contents

Note to the Reader

Three views from c.2600BC

In *A New Philosophy of Literature* Nicholas Hagger traced the fundamental theme of world literature back to c.2600BC, when *The Epic of Gilgamesh* was written.

The three stories, or parables, that follow, written in 1963, 2005 and 2020, purport to predate the fundamental theme in c.2600BC, when the Great Pyramid was built. They report the bafflement of an official who has worked at Giza for 29 years and sees the Great Pyramid as an empty tomb, a secular folly; then his breakthrough into seeing it as a means for all to become an *akh*, a spiritual soul or Shining One; and finally his realisation that it is a House of Eternity for Khufu as the Sun-god Ra. The official finds himself mirroring Reality after what amounts to a metaphysical quest.

The three accounts from Giza present the secular and metaphysical aspects of the fundamental theme in terms of their source in c.2600BC, before the beginning of world literature, the literary tradition and the evolution of its fundamental theme. (See the Preface.)

A modern 'editor' provides a note and footnotes to the first two accounts, and footnotes to the third account. The Appendix (p.57) and its Notes and References to Sources (p.71) are from a section on the Egyptian Light in Nicholas Hagger's *The Light of Civilization*.

Preface

The Great Pyramid as the Quest for Eternity and as Self-Aggrandising Folly, and the Fundamental Theme of World Literature

What inspired my interest in the Great Pyramid
These three stories were inspired by events in my adolescence that got me interested in the Egyptian Pharaohs.

When I was ten my dentist was Dr Carter, the brother of Howard Carter who discovered Tutankhamun's tomb in November 1922. He was bespectacled and silver-haired, and he had a surgery in Loughton High Road, within walking distance of where I was living in Station Road, Loughton. In those days teeth were drilled without a prior injection, and to make the pain more bearable he told me stories about the finding of the tomb. He would say, "And then, my brother turned the corner and saw…. Open wide." And after more drilling, "… A wonderful golden mask from the 14th century BC." He told me about the curse associated with the tomb, an inscription on a stone that guarded it: "To whomsoever shall disturb these remains, death shall come on swift wings." (Or: "Death shall come on swift wings to him who disturbs the peace of the pharaoh.") And how Lord Carnarvon, who financed the dig, had died of a mosquito bite in Cairo on 5 April 1923. I was spellbound by the boy Pharaoh, his early death and the discovery of his tomb in the Valley of the Kings, and looked for books in my local library that would deepen my knowledge of ancient Egypt.

When I was fifteen I was given an original figurine of Tutankhamun. One of the masters at Chigwell School, George Harvey Webb ("Spider Webb"), was very eccentric. He had done many things in his life, which he told us about. He claimed to have been a monk in Armenia and a Romanian spy, and to have walked into Buckingham Palace in German uniform during the Second World War to test its security – and reached the first floor before he was challenged. He married a millionairess dancer and got through £2 million and, in penury, lived in a caravan in the school grounds. He was extremely knowledgeable, he coped with all the Latin and Greek set books unseen, knowing all the meanings of all the words in his head, and he kept the bookloft.

One day, rooting round some classical texts in the dimly-lit bookloft, which was a large attic, I came across a glass case of Egyptian figurines and, the only boy there, asked, "Sir, do you want these?" He said, "No, they have Tutankhamun's curse on them. They came from his tomb. When I was in Egypt in 1922 and Howard Carter was working in the tomb

Wooden *shawabti* **of Tutankhamun**

I found them on the sand – and they have brought me nothing but ill luck. If you are not superstitious you can have them." Astonished I said, "Oh, thank you sir," and, holding the glass case carefully in front of me, I scampered down the stairs and ran out to the bicycle shed and put it in my saddle-bag and later cycled home with the case and its contents.

I had a perfect wooden *shawabti* (funerary figurine) of Tutankhamun, two wooden effigies of gods (one of Horus) and many small figurines of gods with animal heads and a figure of Osiris, all a little larger than toy soldiers. The figurine of Tutankhamun, my lifelong companion, has no pupils in its eyes, but when I look at it in semi-dark the eyes strangely seem to have pupils. It was carved to show pupils within the darkness of the tomb.

The Great Pyramid of Khufu

The Great Pyramid had haunted me for some while. The more I read about it the more it baffled me. Its building had involved tens of thousands for (it was generally agreed) more than 30 years, and as the sarcophagus was empty no one was certain that it was a tomb, and no one seemed to know why it had been built.

And I was puzzled by Khufu, who built the Great Pyramid (and, according to a papyrus in Saqqara, also the lion-man the Greeks in Alexander the Great's time called the Sphinx). There is only one tiny ivory statue of him in the Museum of Egyptian Antiquities in Cairo,

The tiny ivory figurine of Khufu found at Abydos, with Khufu's Horus name Her-Mejedu inscribed on the throne

7.5 cms (3 inches) high, and we know it is of Khufu as it has his Horus name, Her-Mejedu, inscribed on his throne. For the evidence as to the length of his reign, see the Historical Note on p.55. For the length of Khafra's reign, see the Historical Note on Khafra on p.56.

By general consent Khufu was the most powerful man who ever lived as he was able to dragoon a nation into building the Great Pyramid for at least three decades. He had a team that organised the work very impressively and had the workers living near the Great Pyramid for decades, and farmers supplemented them during the months when the Nile flooded their fields. And while all this was going on, Khufu, it is now clear, regarded himself as the Sun-god, the lord of the universe (see the Appendix, pp.64–65). He claimed to be the sun, and if it was he who began the lion-man looking for the sun on the horizon it was because he regarded himself as lord of all.

According to the Turin papyrus, which can be dated 1,400 years after the Great Pyramid's construction, Khufu reigned for 23 years. In his study of the reigns of the early pyramid builders Rainer Stadelmann concluded that he reigned for longer than this. Mark Lehner in *The Complete Pyramids* (the American University in Cairo Press), p.108, reckoned that even if Khufu only reigned 32 or 33 years, the combined mass of the stones involved in the construction work – 2.7 million cubic metres (95.35 million cubic feet) for his pyramid, the causeway, two temples, a satellite pyramid, the queen's pyramids and officials' *mastaba*s – would mean that 230 cubic metres (8,122 cubic feet) of massive granite and limestone blocks would have to be put in place every day.

The limestone blocks on the eastern face of the Great Pyramid, one of which would have had to be put in place every two or three minutes if Khufu's reign was only 32 or 33 years, suggesting that his reign was longer.

This would work out at an average-size block being put in place every two or three minutes in a ten-hour day. The Great Pyramid has about 2.3 million blocks of stone, each of which weighs about 2.5 tons. The nine-metre-long granite slabs that form the ceiling of the Grand Gallery (the passage) weigh 50–80 tons.

When all this is taken into account, it is likely that Khufu reigned much longer than 32 or 33 years. According to one view Khufu reigned for 46 years. The dates traditionally attributed to the building of the Great Pyramid – c.2604–2581BC or 2551–2528BC (see the Appendix, p.64) – are therefore probably not right. Different chronological systems have been proposed, and there is no widespread agreement, but it can be said that Khufu flourished c.2600BC and the years that followed, at the dawn of recorded history. These three stories contain the details of how the Great Pyramid is thought to have been built.

The Great Pyramid as a symbol of purposelessness

I waited a long time for my appointment to lecture in Japan at two universities to be confirmed. I was interviewed by the British Council on 8 May 1973, and, having lived off my savings in Iraq and now desperate for money, down to my last £8 and wanting to study growing things, I took a job as an LCC labourer on 5 shillings an hour in Dulwich Park, near where I was living. I was now a park gardener. It was a hot summer and I worked from 8 to 5 throughout June and July, hoeing soil and ground elder round the famous rhododendrons and learning about their life cycle and how they revert to type. I learned about their habits and those of azaleas, begonias, bellis daisies and polyanthus, and studied the activities of seeds, of germinations and sproutings, the rhythm of life, the conditions that best bring plants and shrubs to bloom.

It was hard, back-breaking, mindless work – sometimes I had to dig a long trench with a fork in great heat – but the discipline did me good. I had only half-grasped that I had embarked on a purging of myself, a purgation of my lower ego and its senses, and that it was like being in a monastery and tilling fields all day. In the evenings, worn out, I attempted to write, and early on, on Saturday 8 June 1963, I wrote the first version of 'The Riddle of the Great Pyramid' between 4.30 and 6. It was about the apparent purposelessness of the toil that built the Great Pyramid, comparing my own back-breaking efforts with those of the slaves who built the Great Pyramid.

On 17 July 1963, I took my Tutankhamun to Sotheby's, where an expert examined it. He pronounced it genuine but the crucial gold lettering of the Pharaoh's name had rubbed off the bitumen at the back.

Later I was moved to three schools in Dulwich, and for a while was a gardener at what is now Rosendale Primary School, Langbourne Primary School (off Bowen Drive) and Kingsdale Foundation School, and from the grounds watched pupils rush around in their playground at lunchtime. With hindsight I was being shown my future, as I now own four schools in Essex and East London which have 330 staff. Providence had placed me to look at three schools and absorb a subliminal message regarding my future, just as in the park I was taught how to hold my own with school gardeners and the growth of plants and shrubs.

Later still, as the weather got cold, I changed jobs and worked in Dulwich library within walking distance of where I was living, and one day W.B. Emery, the bespectacled Egyptologist, came in, and the librarian introduced me. One day as I walked back from work, I encountered him in Alleyn Road, and stopped him and told him about 'The Riddle of the Great Pyramid'. I asked him why he thought the Great Pyramid was built, and was pleased he did not know. Many years later I found out that Emery had discovered a Sarapeum-like labyrinth among the 1st-dynasty Egyptian tombs: the first evidence for the bull cult. I had seen the Great Pyramid as a symbol of the purposelessness of work, and Emery had not contradicted me.

The Great Pyramid as a symbol of an akh, a shining soul

In November I flew to Japan with my wife and daughter, and on the tarmac at the foot of the aircraft's steps was greeted by four Professors in tails near a huge limousine, one of whom called me "Professor Hagger". It was only then that I realised I was their new Invited Foreign Professor at two universities.

In Japan I embarked on a Mystic Way that would lead to a centre-shift, a glimpse of the sun-like Light, full illumination and unitive consciousness (as can be read in *A Mystic Way* and *My Double Life 1: This Dark Wood*, which set the above experiences within the wider context of my inner development). It would also lead me to an appreciation of the historical Egyptian Light (see the Appendix, an update of what first appeared in *The Fire and the Stones* in 1991). The Japanese mounted an exhibition of treasures from Tutankhamun's tomb in a museum, and on 8 October 1965 I saw the golden death-mask of Tutankhamun for the first time.

In 1970 I visited Egypt alone, from Libya, at a time when there was a blackout because of possible Israeli air attacks. I took a room in Cairo overlooking the Nile and watched the dorsal fins of the dhows on the river. I went to the Pyramids and spent a day studying the Great Pyramid from every angle. I walked round it and up to the King's Chamber. I stood and looked at the Great Pyramid, thinking of my story 'The Riddle of the Great Pyramid', and imagined being the official who was baffled by why it was being built.

I also went to Memphis and the necropolis at Saqqara. I went down to Luxor and visited the Valley of the Kings and Tutankhamun's tomb.

By 1978 I had undergone a development within myself, and from my own experience of illumination I understood the Egyptian *akh* (see Appendix). My interest in Egypt deepened when I met Maurice Blake at a conference in that year. He told me he regressed people to their former lives, and offered to regress me if I visited him in Norwich. I was slightly apprehensive: would there be lasting effects and damage from being hypnotised? But like Goethe's Faust I sought beyond the threshold of death, and I decided this was an opportunity I should not refuse.

I visited him twice, and during the second visit (on 31 August 1978), with a tape-recorder playing, I was taken back to a life in which I surfaced under a huge temple statue of a man I pronounced to be "Ramesses the Second as a Sun-god". I was a woman and laid a garland at his feet at the top of some steps. I lived in the temple. I saw a philosopher sitting outside in the warm sun on a stool, his feet on the sand, naked above the waist with a black beard. I was one of a group of ten temple-maidens sitting before him. I could see what I was wearing: a white dress with one shoulder bare and sandals with a twined thong between each big and second toe. It was all so vivid I could almost put my hand into what I was seeing and pick up a handful of sand.

I knew that we maidens took part in a public ritual involving the Sun-god. This involved Ramesses II coming into the temple and choosing one of us to take part in the ritual to make the Nile flood.

Then I was at the beginning of such a ceremony. It was a hot day with a blue sky, and those who lived in the temple were on parade, and I saw the young Ramesses arrive, wearing a tall and shining gold head-dress and gold armour. He was surrounded by his entourage and we were thrilled to see him. He looked magnificent. He came down the line and stopped at me and touched his heart, and I dissolved into tears on tape, looking with emotion at the honour for I was "the chosen one" and he would take me with him and make the Nile flood. My name was Nebhotep, and I was ecstatically happy. (There is more about the regression in *The Promised Land*, where I give the reason for believing that the large temple statue was the one Shelley wrote about in 'Ozymandias'.)

I still do not know if this was a day-dream, an imagining, or whether it was a far memory of my encounter with Ramesses II. But to me it feels as if I have a memory of ancient Egypt more than a thousand years after the building of the Great Pyramid. I also have a memory from that regression of a young lady with black hair and a long white dress – me – standing by a lily-pond with waist-high papyrus reeds.

I was by now imbued with the Egyptian culture. Eleven months before that regression, in 1977, I had attended dances (choreographed from hieroglyphic records by Dennis Stoll) by five Egyptian temple-dancers, and it was extraordinary that one of them, Christine Finlayson, later Klein, would dance at the launch of my book *The Fire and the Stones* in 1991 and make a pyramid from her sloping arms, fingers meeting above her head to suggest that the pyramid shape was the rays not just of the sun but of the Light, the view in my historical account of the Egyptian Light, which she was then presenting, which appeared in *The Fire and the Stones* in 1991 and was updated in *The Light of Civilization* in 2006 (see the Appendix).

By 2005, when I next went to Egypt – I visited Sharm El-Sheikh, Luxor and Cairo, and again spent time at the Great Pyramid, I walked up to the King's Chamber and the empty sarcophagus – I was brimming with the spiritual meaning of the Great Pyramid, which I had covered in *The Fire and the Stones*. The Great Pyramid was now a place where the central theme of Egyptian religion could be re-enacted and transmitted among Egyptians: for the *ka*, or double, to become an *akh*, a spiritual soul that is filled with Light from the beyond, and become a Shining One with an illuming *akh*. (See Appendix.) This new view drew on *The Book of the Dead* and saw the seeking of the Sun-god Ra as having an esoteric side: the mystic opening to the Light so the soul might become an *akh*.

I wrote the second story, 'The Meaning and Purpose of the Great Pyramid', in the airport departure lounge, waiting for my return flight. I worked on the story during the flight.

The Great Pyramid as a House of Eternity
I visited Egypt in 2020 after visiting Jordan (as recounted in *The Promised Land*). I went to Luxor, and in the Temple of Karnak on 8 March 2020 noticed a recurrent hieroglyph of a pyramid on a column. I spoke to the guide about it. He told me the pyramid was the hieroglyphic symbol for eternity, not a tomb symbolising death, and suddenly I had a revelation. The Great Pyramid was a House of Eternity. I had used that phrase at the end of the passage in the Appendix before 1991, and I now had a new interpretation of the purpose of the Great Pyramid.

I wrote in my diary for that day:

Luxor. Up at 6.15, breakfasted to leave by 8am for Karnak.... The plant and bee, lower and upper Egypt, with pyramid = eternity and the ankh long life.... Talked with the guide Nojat about the pyramid meaning eternity and not the tomb (death). All Egyptians believed in the next life. Talked about 'The Riddle of the Great Pyramid' and its sequel. The secret of the Great Pyramid is that it is a tomb where you could find eternity, the second life, and so it is a symbol of eternity as is the hieroglyphic: the gateway to the second life. So I have a third instalment, written by the same man who is now old and understands at last, but what has happened to Khufu in the meantime? The Sphinx is Khufu [compare the pictures on pp.8 and 44] – about 20 years ago one of the graves in Saqqara had a papyrus stating that Khufu built the Sphinx, a lion with the king's head. I have a trilogy which can appear in one book.... All three in a book *The Building of the Great Pyramid*.

I visited the Great Pyramid again on 10 March 2020, and it was then that I saw the likeness between Khafra and the lion-man the Greeks called the Sphinx (see four pictures on p.44), and finally disregarded the papyrus in Saqqara stating that Khufu built the lion-man. He may have built it, but Khafra made sure his own head was on the lion.

Khafra took the name Ra and differed from Khufu, his father. He was under the Sun-god Ra, he did not claim to be Ra. For the possibility that the face of the lion-man was Khafra's, see the Appendix, pp.69–70.

I wrote 'The Great Pyramid as a House of Eternity' on my return to England in the first days of the first lockdown from Covid-19, towards the end of March 2020. The Great Pyramid has now haunted me for 60 years.

In the satirical tradition of Swift

There is a satirical tradition in English prose that goes back to Swift's *A Modest Proposal* and *Gulliver's Travels*. It works by analogy. A first-person narrator recounts a tale that can be preposterous and ridicule – the writer of *A Modest Proposal* recommends that Irish peasants should sell their own children as food for the rich to solve the "problem" of poverty caused by the English Government – or that can expose the workings of the English Government and ridicule, as in *Gulliver's Travels*. The tradition is critical of the English Government of the day. See my essay in an Appendix of *A New Philosophy of Literature*, 'The Theme of *Gulliver's Travels*: How the New Utopia of the Age of Reason is Shipwrecked on the Reality of Human Nature'.

This trilogy is a first-person narration that is at once critical of the Egyptian Pharaoh's long self-aggrandisement in building his tomb to guarantee his second life, and also critical by implication of all societies' organisation of their workers to dubious ends and purpose. It also comments on the project that dominates the working life of each of us. Every government and business involves something major it is trying to achieve. Each government and business is a project that has its own detailed planning, its organisation of its workers, its productivity, its measurable progress and its desired end result which must be assessed. We all have a Pyramid project in our lives. It may be building up a school, it may be building up a profitable business, it may be delivering a Government target, but it is semi-permanently there, overshadowing our lives.

In my case, a lifelong Pyramid has been my construction of Universalism in all disciplines. Hours of research and planning have gone into it, the workers in publishing houses and their copy-editors, designers and printers have been engaged in it, the number of books covering it have been delivered at a certain target rate on my part, the progress can be measured and the desired end result can be assessed. The surrounding methods and criteria of all Pyramid projects in every walk of life and their stages have similarities.

In short, there is something universal as well as satirical in this Swiftian tradition. The Swiftian tradition goes back to Greek and Roman times, to Aristophanes, Juvenal and Menippus of Gadara. There are many writers within this tradition in European culture, including Pope. And in more recent times, Kafka has shown Joseph K battling with bureaucratic decisions and feeling isolated from society, the feeling of Gregor after turning into a cockroach in *Metamorphosis*.

The fundamental theme of world literature

In *A New Philosophy of Universalism* I stated the fundamental theme of world literature as a variation of the dialectical method that runs through all my works, $+A + -A = 0$: a quest for metaphysical Reality and a condemnation of central follies and vices in relation to an implied virtue. The quest for metaphysical Reality can be traced back to the Mesopotamian *The Epic of Gilgamesh*, c.2600BC, and the following of a Mystic Way involving the soul's journey to eternity in awareness of the unity of the universe, and the follies and vices can be traced back to the satirical works of the Greeks and Romans, as we have just seen.

The Great Pyramid's cultural symbolism is that of the quest for metaphysical Reality of the Egyptian *ka* and *akh* seeking eternity in the second life. It is a symbol of eternity, but like all symbols it has layers of meaning that apply at different levels, from social employment to a religious tomb, from an empty cenotaph to an *akh* cathedral, and from the House of the Sun-god to a House of Eternity. The Swiftian satirical tradition condemns the social follies and vices of Governmental thinking and planning behind the symbol, and ridicules self-aggrandisement in relation to an implied virtue: its statement of what is morally good.

All satire involves a condemnation of social follies and vices in relation to an implied virtue. The virtue here is an aligning of the illumined soul (the *akh*) to its second life in eternity, the soul's quest for metaphysical Reality, and the follies and vices are Khufu's self-aggrandisement and egocentric progress to his second life which enslaves a whole nation while it builds a Pyramid that's disproportionately only a symbolic tomb.

14, 21–22 April, 24 May 2021

Nicholas Hagger before the Great Pyramid (left) and the Pyramid of Khafra on 10 March 2020

THREE REPORTS FROM c.2600BC

1

The Riddle of the Great Pyramid

"'Riddle', 'a question or statement testing ingenuity in divining its answer or meaning, a puzzling fact'" (Concise Oxford Dictionary)

I

I have been an official here at Giza for twenty-nine years. Since I have witnessed the whole operation from the first scratch on the sand, I may have some justification for regarding myself as something of an authority on the matter.

Two views of the small statue of Khufu in the Museum of Egyptian Antiquities, Cairo, the only statue of him in existence.

The manner in which the Great Pyramid has been constructed is as follows. As soon as Khufu succeeded as Pharaoh on the death of his father Snefru, work began to prepare the site. The vizier and building manager Prince Hemiunu and his chief architect Mirabu[1] (neither of whom I have ever seen) were heavily involved in the drawings. The builders first drew a line in the sand directed at true north. They then laid out a square with precise right-angles. To strengthen and stabilise the structure a mass of bedrock was incorporated within the square, which prevented the builders from checking the

3

square's accuracy by measuring the diagonals, yet by mathematical calculations they still managed to achieve an unsurpassed degree of precision. As soon as the surveyors had finished marking out the site, news came through that Khufu was anxious to begin work. Accordingly Recruitment Offices were opened in each of the twenty-two provinces (*sepats*) in our land to attract workers with high wages and tax exemptions. Once the workers had been transported here to Giza their first task was to build the stone compounds. Tented camps were considered and rejected in view of the anticipated length of the project. And so workers were shipped down the Nile to the granite quarries [at Aswan, ed.] and across the Nile to the limestone quarries on the east bank [at Tura as well as on the Giza plateau, ed.] and under my direction (I am Superintendent and Controller of Compounds) they hewed granite blocks and limestone casing blocks from the quarries, levered them on to rollers, dragged them to the river, floated them up or across on rafts and dragged them to the sites appointed by the surveyors.

This process continued for three years before any start was made on the actual project. In due course the compounds will be demolished. Once a suitable number of workers were housed, work began on the levelling of the plateau and on the laying out of the base of the Great Pyramid with knotted ropes. At the same time more workers made a road to the high-water mark of the Nile. Altogether this took a further ten years, and during this time reinforcements were constantly arriving and building more stone compounds round the plateau. Only when all this had been done did work begin on the Great Pyramid.

The plan, as conceived by the architects, was simple. Workers were to achieve the shape that Khufu wanted by laying blocks all over the square base and then by piling on further layers until they tapered to one block at the top. They were to get the blocks into position by building ramps of wet sand, mud-bricks and stones which were to be lengthened and mounded up as each new layer was reached so that the gradients remained constant, and by using rollers and levers when dragging the blocks up the ramps. The sides of the Great Pyramid beneath the ramps would therefore be a series of small steps. When the top was reached, triangular casing blocks were to be fitted into position to give a sloping effect. Thus, four casing blocks would meet in a point at the top, and thereafter there would be enough to fill in all the steps. And as the casing was to be built downwards, so the ramps would be dismantled downwards. And this is the position today, sixteen years after the first block of the Great Pyramid was laid into place: we have just begun the casing.

For the last sixteen years the organisation of labour has been based on the principle of four annual shifts of three months each. Although, therefore, a total of 400,000 unskilled workers work on the Great Pyramid during one year, at any one time there are only 100,000, and for their shift, they are paid what elsewhere would be six months' wages and exempted from one year's taxes. By this means enthusiasm and morale are maintained all the year round and only a minimum of compounds are required. The 100,000 workers are apportioned equally on the east and west sides of the Nile. On the east side 20,000 mine the quarries, and 30,000 haul the blocks to the river, float them across, and deliver them to the masons. On the west side 30,000 haul the blocks from the masons to the ramps, and 20,000 work on the ramps and lend a hand with the gruelling work of dragging the blocks up the ramps. Yet so delicate is the organisation that each block is staggered in relation to the others so as to avoid congestion on the ramps.

This staggering is achieved by the "Hundred Gang System", whereby the miners, the haulers, the masons and the ramp-workers are each composed of 100 gangs, and gang 1 of each handles the same block throughout, as do gangs 2, 3, and 4, and so on up to 100.

Consider the complications of this system. On the east side, for example, there are two conditions of labour: that the miners should produce 100 blocks a week, and that the haulers should take no more than one week (168 hours) in dragging each block to the river, in floating it across and in delivering it to the masons, although each block weighs some two and a half tons. Now the miners work in gangs of 100, and two gangs to a block, gangs 1A and 1B – one on, one off. And the haulers work in gangs of 150, and two gangs to a block, gangs 1A and 1B – one on, one off. Nevertheless, somehow there is a gap of one hour between the time that miners 1A and 1B hand over their block to haulers 1A and 1B, and the time that miners 2A and 2B hand over their block to haulers 2A and 2B. And what is more, each gap is seen in relation to the state of the Nile in about 160 hours' time. And moreover, this gap is maintained throughout the year in spite of the end of annual shifts and the beginning of new ones, and in spite of the fact that each block, although roughly cut, must be of the correct measurement, for miners 1A and 1B are acting on the conveyed instructions of gang 1 of the masons, and so on.

Indeed, the slightest delay could destroy the whole co-ordination. For consider with regard to the masons: each casing block must arrive at the masons' yard in the order in which it is expected, just as, another 168 hours later, it must leave the masons' yard in the order in which it arrived. This co-ordination is effected in this way. There are 1,000 masons, and they work in 100 gangs, ten to a block. The block mined by miners gangs 1A and 1B, and hauled by haulers gangs 1A and 1B, goes to masons gang 1, and the second block to masons gang 2, and so on. Thus, one hour after gang 100 has completed its (previous week's) block, gang 1 discharges the first block of the new week. But if the block for gang 2 arrives before the block for gang 1 owing to the delay of haulers 1A and 1B, for example, then gangs 2–100 will be delayed while gang 1 waits, for gang 1's casing block must be keyed into the Great Pyramid before gang 2's casing block.

It is to this end that gang 1 has already conferred with the mathematicians and determined the exact measurements and angles of the particular block that is expected, making allowances for any slight discrepancy there may be in one of the blocks on which it will rest. And it is to this end that gang 1 has likewise conferred with the architects and engineers. The masons are craftsmen – each block is to them a masterpiece, they scorn mass-production – and their task is much more complex than merely smoothing the surfaces and marking the blocks with red ink to indicate their place in the structure of the Great Pyramid to the engineers. In view of such care and accuracy there can be no delay. And never yet has there been one error, not in sixteen years.

Consider the scale of the project. I have been told that in all there are 2.3 million stone blocks, which rise to a height of 146.6m.[2] The bottom one weighs 6.18 tons, the top one 2.5 tons. The blocks over the Upper Chamber weigh 50–80 tons yet the greatest difference in length between the four 230m sides of the Great Pyramid is only 4cms (2ins). Thousands of craftsmen have been involved in this astonishing project, which has built the world's highest building.[3]

Who is responsible for so elaborate an organisation? Certainly credit for maintaining the flow of blocks in their correct order must go to the officials, to the Directors and Inspectors of Mathematics, Engineering, Architecture and Stonemasonry in the beginning, and, under their expert direction, to the Directors and Inspectors of Production and Design, to the Directors of Haulage, to the Directors of Navigation, and to the Directors and Inspectors of Ramps. Nor must the contribution of the foremen be overlooked. But it must be remembered that there could have been no flow of blocks at all in the first place without the initial plan, and that the officials (very completely, to be sure) are merely following the instructions of the Pyramid Committee, as are all of us who are engaged in this operation.

Little is known about the Pyramid Committee. Its messages and commands come through remote and devious channels, and were it not for the evidence of the complexity of the organisation of this project it might even be possible to doubt its existence. For some years, ever since the levelling of the plateau, in fact, there has been some speculation as to its location, and rumour has it variously that the Pyramid Committee resides on the forbidden western side of the Great Pyramid, or in a large palace near Memphis. (It is of course well known that the west is associated with death and the east with life, so it is only natural and appropriate that the western side should be forbidden to workers.) By now the rumours have become legends, and the legends conflict, and all that can be said with certainty is that somewhere, doubtless surrounded by all the most modern equipment, it bears the incessant responsibility of the highest command, together with the foreknowledge of the horrible consequences of so much as one error or oversight. For it is well known that the Pyramid Committee is directly responsible to none other than Khufu himself, the most powerful god-man the world has ever seen or will ever be likely to see.

The only existing statue of Khufu, showing his features

II

But the organisation is far from being entirely economic. For every official engaged in the production and distribution of blocks there is another official engaged in the direction of the workers' welfare. Here on the south side of the Great Pyramid reside the Directors and Inspectors of Food, Clothing, and Working Conditions, the Directors of Public Health and Free-Time Education, and the Directors of Letters and River Transport – not to mention the Directors of Admissions and Departures, the Director of Roll Calls and the Director of Personnel Problems. Furthermore, each official has a clerical staff of the magnitude of any government office in any of the provinces, and whole armies of scribes often work far into the night to keep abreast of the work.

Consider the Directorate of Accounts, for example. The Pyramid Committee wisely foresaw that if workers were paid at Giza there would be robberies. On completion of their annual three-month shift, therefore, the workers return to their provinces and collect their wages from their local Recruitment Office, and the pay-days are staggered to avoid congestion. Four times a year, therefore, the Directorate of Accounts must complete the necessary forms for 100,000 men (taking account of any absences without leave) and ensure that each form reaches the correct Recruitment Office in the correct province. And what is more, each form must be accompanied by a Certificate of Tax Exemption, which must be signed by the Director of Accounts himself. And furthermore the returns to the Pyramid Committee must be accurate to the last scratch on a tablet.

The social conditions of the workers, then, are good. They live 50 to a compound, so there are 1,000 compounds by the quarries on the east side of the Nile and 1,000 compounds on the north side of the Great Pyramid on the west side of the Nile. They work a ten-hour day and a five-and-a-half-day week, and during the hot months they are permitted a siesta and make up the time in the comparative cool of the evenings. At the end of the day's stint the haulers return to their compounds, no matter how near the river or the ramps they may be, and there they are fed with lentils, leeks, radishes, onions, garlic and bread, and if for some reason one compound is to hold a celebration, then wine is provided free of charge.

Ruins of workers' settlement

And it is likewise with the miners, the masons and the ramp-workers. If during the day any worker has suffered what he considers to be an injustice at the hands of an official, then he can go to one of the Workers' Brotherhoods – there is one on either side of the river – for the workers have their own organisation for redressing grievances and ensuring the best conditions.

As regards recreation, the workers have opportunities to play games or hold horse-races, and some attend Free-Time education, though this is not so popular. Otherwise they can walk by the Nile or watch the professional entertainers. It should be added that behind the compounds there are some specially guarded rest-houses, in which visiting wives can stay for a maximum of one week a month, although most workers reconcile themselves to three months' celibacy in the year in return for the rewards they will enjoy with their wages during the remaining nine months.

There is therefore great justice in the organisation, and social reformers have no cause to protest against the foresight and humanitarianism of the Pyramid Committee. Every worker is free – there are no slaves or foreign captives, as there were under Snefru – and there seems to be little to substantiate the rumours which assert that criminals are treated inhumanely on the forbidden western side of the Great Pyramid. Moreover no worker is paid less than the official clerks.

There are admittedly class distinctions: the officials here on the south side of the Great Pyramid and their clerical staff will have little to do socially with the workers on the north side of the Great Pyramid, just as the Pyramid Committee (which is rumoured to have been drawn from the aristocracy) will have nothing to do socially with the officials. But in my experience as Superintendent and Controller of Compounds, this does not unduly worry the workers, who are anyway apt to feel a trifle awkward in the presence of their "social betters". They are content to work for their subsistence and to enjoy their leisure. And they can always console themselves with the thought that, no matter what class distinction there may be, all men engaged on this operation are, without exception, enslaved to the Great Pyramid, and have their lives dominated by it. And that is true from the meanest labourer to the highest authority, Khufu himself.

III

In view of all this it must be admitted that the Pyramid Committee has left nothing to chance. In that case, so much organisation and endeavour must surely be justified by the purpose and value of work? So I thought before the first block of the Great Pyramid was laid, and so I have thought every day for the last sixteen years. Every day I have seen hosts of men in loin-cloths bent double, the ropes chaffing their naked bodies in the hot sun, and every day I have looked up at the Great Pyramid and asked myself 'Why? What's it all for? Surely it has some purpose, some meaning?' For sixteen years I have been reluctant to admit that my question is unanswerable – every day for sixteen years I have duly conducted my own private speculations, and I regret to have to report that even now my conclusion is far from firm.

Consider. The most obvious solution seems to be the religious one, that through the Great Pyramid Khufu's body and *ka* (his double body) will, on his death, allow his *ba* (soul) and *akh* (shining spirit) to find their way to the spirit world in the West, perhaps sailing to Ra (in whom Khufu does not believe) in his solar wooden boat which is to be buried on the southern side of his pyramid, where they will assume the form of Osiris and judge the dead and dwell with Ra in Eternal Sunshine. It is rumoured that one of the Queens' pyramids contains the unmarked tomb of Khufu's mother, Queen Hetepheres, who had her internal organs stored in four compartments of a square alabaster jar, including her lungs. Of course her heart and kidneys were not removed – her heart was of course left in her mummy so it could be weighed in the scales against a feather by Osiris in the Last Judgement. Her body was bound in 100 double arm's lengths (i.e. 100 yards) of linen. If such elaborate mummification practices took place on Khufu's mother, how could they not have taken place on Khufu? We all know that Khufu is now the main god, that there is a local divine cult of Khufu at Giza, that he belongs to the horizon, is *akhty* (a Shining One) and has taken the place of Ra. Traditionally Khepri is the rising morning sun in the east, the scarab pushing the sun like a dung-beetle rolling a ball of dung; Ra is the sun at midday; and Atum is the setting evening sun. Perhaps this pyramid is to reflect one or all of these with its shining casing stones, when they are in place – even though Khufu has not taken the name of, and therefore does not believe in, Ra. It is dangerous – seditious – to confess this, but I personally do not believe in the spirit world in the West, or in the *ka*, or in the resurrection of the body after this life, or, indeed, in any of the Horus-Osiris or Ra/Sun-god legends which pass as our national religion, but I of course believe that Khufu is a god and if Khufu believes in them, then at least the Great Pyramid makes sense. On the other hand, even if Khufu does believe in them, why the necessity to build a Pyramid? Why not merely an ordinary burial chamber, a *mastaba* – a luxurious *mastaba* of course, but a *mastaba* of the conventional shape?

According to the priests the conditions for attaining the spirit world are relatively simple. Neither *ka* nor body will survive unless they are incarcerated in a tomb. If the body is to survive there must, in addition, be mummification, and to guard against the possibility that mummification may fail to preserve the body, there should be a statue of the body to stand in the body's stead should the need arise. And in addition, if the *ka* is to survive, offerings must be brought to the tomb.

Nowhere do the priests assert that the Pyramid form is a condition for attaining the spirit world. Nowhere do they assert that the Pyramid is shaped like rays from the sun bursting through cloud, up which Khufu will travel to reach Eternal Sunshine. Nor is there any evidence to suggest that the Pyramid form is astronomical in its origins, or that the fact that the entrance is on the north face is to be associated with the imperishable Pole Star or circumpolar stars. Nor indeed is there any evidence to suggest that Khufu himself is to be associated with the imperishable Pole Star. If, as is rumoured, there is an alignment with particular stars this is unbeknown to us, the builders of the Great Pyramid. It is rumoured that there will be more pyramids to replicate three stars close together,[4] but we dismiss this as fanciful. There is no precedent or evidence for such a view. In the past we believed that the circumpolar stars are eternal as they never dip below the horizon, but the change from worship of the lunar night sky to sun-worship happened two hundred years ago with Pharaohs of the second dynasty – for example Nebra and Neferkara – who took the name Ra long before Khufu's reign.

Perhaps then the Pyramid form is to protect the burial chamber against thieves? But will it afford any protection at all? For the Pyramid has a door, like any burial chamber, and the door cannot be permanently sealed because of the offerings which must be laid in the chamber. Moreover, the two air-channels for the Upper Chamber – one to the north and one to the south – are not for a *ka*, which does not need air to survive. There may theoretically be a link between the air-holes on the north side and Khufu's journey to the northern stars, but there has never been a tradition linking Khufu's *ba* or *akh* to the southern stars. Nor could they have been left for Sokar, god of the underworld, for it is well known that gods do not breathe or need air. In fact, the air-holes are not really air-holes at all. Strangely, though the mouths of these two air-holes in the Upper Chamber are open (as I have seen with my own eyes), the passages bend and are blocked – I am told on excellent authority – by stones a finger long (i.e. 8cms), so the air-flow stops at them and does not reach the Pyramid's outer casing which, I am reliably informed, was always going to cover the outer walls where the "air-holes" might have come out. The work to achieve these two "air-holes", and the two in the Lower Chamber, has been very complicated – a builder's nightmare – and yet no one knows why this complication has been necessary.

Consider again, if Khufu were so eager to preserve his *ka* and his body, why did he close the temples and forbid the priests to make sacrifices or make statues of him? And why did he place himself above the high priest and our religion and declare himself a god, "*Khut*", "Glory"? The official explanation is that the poor in our land have been harassed by burdensome temple dues (and of that there is no doubt), and that Khufu, although of course believing in our national religion, is a realist – a humanitarian, not a tyrant. But however commendable his action may be to an atheist or a progressive reformer, there is no denying the fact that Khufu has made enemies of the very priests who will sacrifice and make offerings to his *ka* when he lies within the Great Pyramid. For unless the priests make sacrifices they cannot live.

It would seem, then, that – in spite of the official explanation – Khufu does not in fact believe in the spirit world. In any event, there is certainly no religious reason for the size of the Great Pyramid, and none that I can see for its shape. And its purpose is a mystery in religious terms, for there is no certainty that when finished it will actually be used as a tomb.

Surely, therefore, there are secular reasons for the function and form of the Great Pyramid?

Does history throw any light on the matter? So far as the form is concerned, our historians see the Great Pyramid as the culmination of a tradition that began with Zoser's stepped pyramid at Saqqara and continued with Snefru's half-stepped, half-smooth pyramid and the first to have any form of casing, his Red Pyramid, which were both at Medum. (Snefru, Khufu's father, did not take the name Ra, and Khufu followed him in this. Did the pyramid form have something to do with his not being a follower of Ra?) According to one of our leading architects, the Pyramid Committee issued instructions to the effect that the form of the pyramid at Medum was to be pushed to its logical conclusion. But why? Merely to follow an architectural tradition?

Unfortunately, in all my research – and research is treated with suspicion here and discouraged, for it may be seen as questioning and deemed seditious – I have been unable to discover what led Zoser and Snefru to chance upon the forms they did. And so long as this crucial question remains in obscurity, it would appear that the problem of the form is insoluble.

So far as the function is concerned, the Great Pyramid does not fit into this historical tradition. In fact Khufu has confused this historical tradition. For everyone knows that, for all their tyranny, both Zoser and Snefru were deeply religious men who even went so far as to increase the temple dues. Their tombs, if not the pyramids which enclose them, were built for eschatological reasons, unlike (as it would seem) the burial chamber in the Great Pyramid. Nor does the Great Pyramid fit into the tradition that began with Zoser's pyramid and Snefru's second pyramid at Dahshur. For it is well known that the pyramids at Medum and Dahshur are cenotaphs. It may seem that there is good reason for believing that the Great Pyramid is also a cenotaph as the sarcophagus in the Upper Chamber is too wide to pass through the entrance to the chamber and was dragged up the ramp and placed in position while the stones round it were being raised and was then enclosed from above. I saw this with my own eyes.

Sarcophagus in the upper chamber in the Great Pyramid

As tradition dictates that the Pharaoh should be dragged to his burial chamber in his sarcophagus, there was clearly never any intention to use the Upper Chamber as a burial chamber. The same may be true of the two lower chambers. No one knows why there are three in all – one underground and two above ground. Did Khufu plan to be buried in the subterranean lower chamber, then change his mind and introduce a second chamber with two air-holes above it, and then change his mind again and build the Upper Chamber with two air-holes? It is seditious to believe that Khufu, who is a god, could change his mind, and it is inconceivable that in all this meticulous planning and precision of execution the project should turn out to be so haphazard that one, let alone two, changes of mind could take place. And so, it may be thought, the Great Pyramid must be a cenotaph.

Nevertheless, the Great Pyramid cannot be a cenotaph, for a cenotaph is, by definition, an empty tomb and, say what you will, the Great Pyramid contains a burial chamber which no one doubts Khufu himself will one day occupy although there has never been any confirmation of this and there are actually good reasons for believing otherwise. Why make not just one but three burial chambers if there was no intention of using them for burial and if they are to remain empty tombs? Why all this gigantic labour to produce an empty tomb? Why, his mother Queen Hetepheres was buried in a tomb on the eastern side of the Great Pyramid, suggesting that Khufu *will* one day be laid to rest in one of the three burial chambers here.

Furthermore, it is traditional for the Pharaoh to have 23 statues of himself in his mortuary temple near his pyramid, one for each of the 22 provinces which themselves reflect the 22 parts of Osiris's body when it was torn to pieces, before Isis collected them and reassembled them. Will Khufu not follow the tradition? He is, after all, King of Upper and Lower Egypt, and a symbol of all the provinces.

Could it not be, then, that the Great Pyramid bears no functional relation to any historical tradition, and is to be regarded as a secular memorial, an enduring monument by which Khufu's people will remember him after he is dead? A cartouche in the wall of the highest of the five tiered chambers above the Upper Chamber says (according to a workman who has seen it and informed me): "Wonderful is the White Crown of Khufu" (meaning the crown of Upper Egypt). It is common knowledge that Khufu refers to the Great Pyramid as "*Khut*" or "Glory" – could not this "Glory" be an expression of his temporal power, and does it not tower to a height of 480 feet over the desert solely to subjugate all visible nature from the east to west?

For ten years, I must admit, I thought this interpretation to be the most likely. There was one main objection, of course. No matter what the priests say – and they have an axe to grind – Khufu cannot be a tyrant. He is a god, after all, and all his speculations are therefore divine. And would a man as progressive as he evidently is spend twenty-nine years in subjecting so many of his people to so egoistic a task? Would a man whose concern for social justice is to be seen everywhere yield so totally to the pomps and vanities of temporal power? I did not think so. And, as subsequent events have shown, I am sure I have been proved right.

Perhaps, then, there are economic reasons? Perhaps Khufu conceived of the operation as a convenient means of ensuring full employment while at the same time completing the necessary task of building what he would regard as his secular tomb? As evidence for this there is the convention, which has been consistently upheld throughout the last sixteen years, that the annual shift of three months which coincides with the inundation of the Nile should be devoted exclusively to the peasants, who would otherwise be idle.

But if so, are there not more constructive ways of obtaining full employment than by building a Great Pyramid merely for the sake of building it? Throughout the twenty-two provinces in our land one could devise dozens of projects which would not only absorb all our labour, both skilled and unskilled, but which would furthermore benefit all sections of our people materially, and raise their standard of living. And if so, why the necessity for so vast and delicate an organisation based on the principle of saving time?

The whole organisation of this project suggests that it has a purpose. Yet an economic interpretation of this project suggests that it has no purpose. And furthermore, if the Great Pyramid is purely economic in its conception, then Khufu himself cannot believe it has a purpose. And who can believe in a purpose if Khufu, the highest authority, who we all know is a god, does not believe in one?

But there is another possibility. Perhaps Khufu believed in the spirit world and the *ka* when he began this project, before he became the god that all now worship. There is some doubt as to the exact year in which he first closed the temples, but most agree that it was some time after the first block of the Great Pyramid was laid. If so, then perhaps he intended the Great Pyramid to have a religious purpose when he began this project, and has subsequently lost interest.

There is some evidence for this. First, although he is officially supposed to make frequent tours of inspection throughout our land, no one I know has ever seen him. He is reputed to remain remote from us in the capital, Memphis, and, surrounded by his scribes, to direct this project from the seclusion of his palace there. Everyone quakes at the mere mention of his name and hastens to praise his glory, yet no one has had the slightest confirmation that he is remotely interested in our work. Indeed, were it not blasphemous and seditious to suggest it openly, one might reasonably suppose that he does not exist, that he is an invention on the part of the Pyramid Committee. I personally am inclined to believe in his existence, for the Pharaoh-tradition has now, so our historians tell us, reached the Fourth Dynasty since King Aha (Menes) united Upper and Lower Egypt, and in view of the weight of the past, no matter how clandestine the Pyramid Committee might be, our land could not change suddenly from a Kingdom into a Republic without anyone among the middle and lower classes knowing anything about it.

Three views of the Great Pyramid

The fact remains, however: if he does exist, no one I know has seen him. Somewhere he bears the responsibility of the highest command, but where? On the forbidden western side of the Great Pyramid? In Memphis? No one I know knows for sure. And just because no one seems to have seen him, he would not, it might be argued, attract attention when he makes his visits of inspection. But is this likely? Would not such a visit of inspection be regarded as a State occasion – would he not be accompanied by his Pyramid Committee and follow the proud fingers of the Committee members as they explain the minute detail with which they have carried out his instructions?

In any event there has been no such occasion. Word would soon get round if there had. And this in itself suggests that he has lost interest. Moreover it has been rumoured that the chief architect, Mirabu, has died, and that his replacement has become rather slapdash of late. I myself have seen no visible evidence of the blocks failing to fit – it is not my job to watch the keying in – and I have heard no rumours to that effect, but half a millimetre would be sufficient proof. And half a millimetre cannot be detected with the naked eye, and the mathematicians are not sociable men. The enthusiasm of the masons and the engineers, of the mathematicians and the architects has not changed, but the crucial question is, have their measurements changed?

There is, however, one major objection to this interpretation. If Khufu exists, and if he has in fact lost interest in the Great Pyramid, why has the organisation and the labour been allowed to continue unchecked as regards its timing? Is it not inconceivable that a man as just as Khufu actually consents to our being merely the anachronism of his will?

Then there is the matter of the huge human-faced lion[5] that has recently gone up out of blocks left over from the Great Pyramid and existing rock. No one knows what this means. A huge face looking to the east must be the Sun-god. But Khufu did not take the name of Ra and opposed the priests of the Sun-god. I have never seen Khufu but I have seen the small statue shown to me in Abydos, which is minute – less than a little finger's length. It is impossible to say whether the rock-face bears Khufu's features but it is possible that it does. Does it show Khufu as Sun-god? Does it show Khufu saying "I am the Sun-god" and asserting his own divinity while watching the rising of Ra? I am now getting into difficult, seditious terrain. Suffice it to say that there has been a lot of speculation among the pyramid-workers as to what the rock-face means and all agree that it actually compounds the mystery at Giza rather than solves it.

In all these suppositions I have failed to mention one vital consideration. What if Khufu should die before the Great Pyramid is finished? Has he bargained for this possible eventuality which would deprive the Great Pyramid of any significance it may have as a tomb? For if he were to die tomorrow, he would probably have to be buried in an ordinary *mastaba* – no one of Khufu's rank can be laid to rest in an incomplete tomb – and, shape and all, the Great Pyramid would have to be abandoned to the elements, unless Khufu's successor were to decide to take over the project for himself.

And so I conclude that the Great Pyramid defies all purpose and meanings. Does this mean that it has no purpose or meaning? All that can be said with certainty is that all this daily organisation and endeavour does not appear to be justified by the purpose and value of the work. But I would go further than that. In fact I would go so far as to maintain that the Great Pyramid would appear to be futile. We are all enslaved to it, yet no one seems to know why, except for Khufu, if he exists, and I doubt whether even he knows, now.

IV

I had my suspicions very early on in this project, but I was unwilling to acknowledge this conclusion. Those were early days, and I assumed there must be some cryptic purpose behind the operation which I did not fully comprehend. I told myself that all this would become clear when the Great Pyramid was finished, and I used to speculate, over my evening drink, as to how the final revelation would come. Would it come in a blinding flash that would leave me thrillingly aglow, or would it come quietly and calmly, perhaps making me a little angry at my stupidity and blindness in not perceiving the answer sooner?

But the years dragged by, and the Great Pyramid showed few signs of being finished, and I became impatient.

Then, ten years ago, I determined to find out what it was all for. Someone must know, I argued. I could not expect an audience with Khufu himself – that would be hoping for too much – but there was a chance that the Pyramid Committee might know. And if they did not know they might be able to find out, they might be able to approach Khufu. So I determined to contact the Pyramid Committee, and that meant going to the Directorate of Publicity, for everyone knows that the only contact with the Pyramid Committee is through Publicity.

Of course I told no one of the action I proposed to take. I flattered myself that I knew my colleagues, my fellow-officials, too well for that. They did not seem to be given to speculation, as I was, and being veritable pillars of society their replies would have been all too predictable. Without exception, they would have been shocked. "Don't interfere," some would have said. "Khufu knows best." Or else: "Worry about your compounds and leave Khufu to worry about the rest." Or: "You mustn't criticise the Committee – the Committee knows what it's doing." But behind their discouragement there would have been a fear: "If you're not careful, Publicity will report you to the Committee." For although Khufu is just, it is well known that he shows no mercy to "rebels who seek to undermine our society". They can be imprisoned for sedition or blasphemy, and what could be more anti-social than to question the whole basis of society here at Giza, the purpose of the Great Pyramid? I was aware of all this, but I had to know. I must confess that I went to Publicity in some trepidation.

The Director of Publicity is of course as much in the dark as the rest of us, and because of his position he is not unnaturally especially sensitive to the question of sedition. Not unnaturally he tried to discourage me. He even went to great lengths to show me all the official slogans in the hopes that my communication would not be necessary. "There is no authority but Khufu." I already knew that. "There is brotherhood before the Great Pyramid." That was of no assistance. "There has been no war since Perabsen." With all due respect, I could not understand how that might be relevant. And so on. At length, however, he reluctantly accepted my short memorandum and agreed to send it through the normal channels to the Pyramid Committee.

For the next few weeks I waited in hope, though I was half afraid that my action might be deemed seditious. Nothing happened. The weeks became months, and a year passed. But still nothing happened. There was nothing I could do to expedite the matter. That would have been most unwise in view of the gravity of my inquiry. So I waited in patience and continued to speculate over my evening drink, and another year passed, and then another, and another.

Eventually I gave up hope of obtaining an answer. My memorandum has been lost, I would tell myself, or else it is waiting in some in-tray beneath a huge stack of papers relating to more immediate problems, the organisation of this project for example. Or perhaps the Pyramid Committee had read my inquiry and deliberately decided that it should receive no answer. Anyhow, as time went on I almost forgot that I had inquired in the first place. In fact I waited ten years.

Then, this morning, quite out of the blue, a servant knocked on my office door and announced that he had been sent by the Director of Publicity. Would I go to Publicity straight away. Even as I stood up, wondering at the urgency of this request, I thought with a sudden hope: 'Perhaps my answer has come.' I hurried excitedly to Publicity, and the Director gravely handed me a large heavy envelope which read: TO THE SUPERINTENDENT AND CONTROLLER OF COMPOUNDS FROM THE PYRAMID COMMITTEE. It was a direct personal communication, and judging by the bulk the Pyramid Committee had replied at some length. This was worth waiting for. Shaking and trembling I tore out the thick papyrus parchment paper and read eagerly: MAN NEEDS THE GREAT PYRAMID. That was all.

The Director of Publicity had done his job. He had other business that required his attention, and he was not going to compromise himself by engaging in a discussion of the riddle. He merely shrugged and said, "The Pyramid Committee always act for the best."

And so I returned to my office bitterly disappointed, and sat down and tried to puzzle the riddle out. Was it a joke – perhaps an official rebuke for my impertinence in asking – or was it a serious reply? The more I pondered, the more I began to suspect that it was in fact a serious reply. I did not think that the Pyramid Committee would jest about a matter of such importance both to them and to Khufu, not to me as a government official. That in itself would be seditious. In that case, what did it mean?

And so I proceeded to reinterpret the interpretations I had tentatively put forward, acting on the assumption that the tone of the missive was serious. I could rule out the religious interpretation for a start. And of the secular interpretations, I could no longer regard the Great Pyramid as a monument to Khufu's worldly power. What was left? The economic interpretation.

To my horror, I began to realise that the economic interpretation might fit the riddle. Why does man need the Great Pyramid? I asked. Evidently because he cannot do without it. Why can't he do without it? The answers began to present themselves. Because the wages are high and he has to subsist. Because work averts boredom. Because his life would be empty without it. Perhaps because all that the Great Pyramid represents has become a habit.

And then I began to have a glimpse of what the Pyramid Committee might mean. "There has been no war since Perabsen" – there is certainly no need to conscript us for military service by using the work here as a form of physical discipline or preparation for fighting battles. Was the Great Pyramid, then, merely a means of channelling off man's peace-time energies? In that case the senselessness of the project was appalling, and neither of my original objections had been answered: why so unconstructive a way of ensuring full employment, and why so time-conscious an organisation?

Nevertheless, there seemed no escaping the conclusion that there was no specific purpose in the construction of the Great Pyramid, save for the incidental purpose that it (allegedly) contained a tomb; the only purpose was to consume man's economic effort.

I was sure of this solution now, as far as one can ever be sure, assuming that the riddle was not intended as a joke, and I immediately began to protest to myself. Man does not need the Great Pyramid, not if he has educated himself to use his leisure profitably. In which case the Great Pyramid is nothing more than a necessary nuisance. Man is not primarily an economic unit in a system. Working for money so debilitates a man that he is too tired to use his leisure profitably. Man ought not to need the Great Pyramid, and Khufu and the Pyramid Committee have based their project on a false view of man. Are Khufu and the Pyramid Committee so out of touch with realities?

And so, after twenty-nine years I have become a rebel. Since this morning I have become so disillusioned with this whole project that I do not think I can ever bear to face the Pyramid-centred conventions of our society again. For one thing, the chief topic of conversation here is the progress of the work, and introductions at social gatherings are invariably accompanied by the question, "What job are you doing on the Great Pyramid?" For another thing, it is the accepted code at social gatherings to invoke Horus, Osiris and Ra, for in spite of the predicament of the priests it is still considered blasphemous to say a word against our national religion, and most of the officials and workers here at Giza still believe that the Great Pyramid has a religious meaning. But I know better, now.

What should I do? Should I tender my resignation to the Director of Departures tomorrow? It would do me no good. I would merely be replaced. One of Publicity's slogans says, "Here no one is indispensable save Khufu", and there are plenty of capable men waiting to be promoted to my position. And then I would have to apply for another job, and I would not be paid one half of what I am earning now, and there would be no tax exemptions. Furthermore, in view of my long service on the Great Pyramid I should have to state the reasons for my resignation in a memorandum, and everyone knows that all memoranda addressed to the Directorate of Departures find their way to the Pyramid Committee through Publicity. And whereas it took the Pyramid Committee ten years to reply to an official inquiry, it might take them only ten minutes to associate my unofficial inquiry with my official resignation, and they might reasonably prefer a charge of sedition against me.

But even though my resignation would do me no good, I would still resign as a protest against the pointlessness of this project if I thought that my act might influence others in our society. However, I am all too aware that my act might have no influence whatsoever. The others are very much on their guard against rebels – in twenty-nine years I have failed to find one kindred spirit – and their attitude is, "If you don't like it, get out of it."

So I shall not resign. Moreover, I do not think I could bring myself to resign, not because I need the Great Pyramid, but because the conundrum it poses has fascinated me for so long that it is now, as it were, part of me. And even though I now feel I am groping towards a certainty, following the communication I received this morning from the Pyramid Committee, I am not absolutely certain why it was intended that man should need the Great Pyramid. Perhaps my interpretation was wrong and man has a non-economic need for the Great Pyramid? One that I have not seen or understood? For all my disillusion, I shall endure to see it completed in the hope that every side of its futile riddle will become clear.

But although the only sane conclusion about the Great Pyramid is a pessimistic one, I do not regard myself as a pessimist. Though I have no religious belief – national religions come and go just as prophets come and go – there are experiences beyond the economic experiences that I enjoy every day. Round the Great Pyramid men laugh and hope for love and choose their futures – men develop their talents and strive and give themselves to the texture of the hard, clear evening sun on the palms by the river. And one can at least be certain of those moments – admiring the universe (as I often do) one can almost forget the primordial symbol of the tomb that (reputedly) towers above all. And perhaps in future times, perhaps in five thousand years from now, men who know the answers will gaze at the finished work and will see it as a monument to our senseless hope and baffled wonderings.

8 June 1963;[6] revised Feb 2005

Editor's Note and Footnotes

"Rainer Stadelmann, in his study of the reigns of the early pyramid builders, concludes that, like his father Sneferu (i.e. Snefru), Khufu reigned longer than the 23 years given him in the Turin papyrus, compiled some 1,400 years later. Even with a reign of 30 to 32 years, the estimated combined mass of 2,700,000cu.m (95,350,000cu.ft) for his pyramid, causeway, two temples, satellite pyramid, three queens' pyramids and officials' *mastabas*, means that Khufu's builders had to set in place a staggering 230cu.m (8,122cu.ft) of stone per day, a rate of one average size block every two or three minutes in a ten-hour day."

Mark Lehner, The Complete Pyramids, p.108.

Herodotus wrote that 100,000 men worked on the Great Pyramid three months at a time for 20 years. Archaeologists such as Petrie found this convincing. (It has recently been conjectured that there were only 25,000–30,000 workers in all, but this is speculation.)

Ancient Egyptians measured length in terms of cubits, i.e. arm lengths (from elbow to thumb-tip), handbreadths (measured on the back across the knuckles) or *setjats* (100 cubits square, approximately two-thirds of an acre). Weight was measured in *debens* (a standard weight of 93.3 grams, though some weights from the Old and Middle Kingdoms appear to have been in units of 12 to 14 grams and sometimes 27 grams). In modern equivalents one metric ton – the Continental tonne – is 1m grams and 1,000 kilos; the English ton is 907,184.7 grams and 907.1847 kilos. All Egyptian measurements have been translated into modern equivalents.

1. Mirabu is mentioned in *Khufu's Wisdom,* a historically researched novel by Egypt's Nobel prizewinner Naguib Mahfouz.
2. Now 138.75m as the capstone is missing.
3. The highest until the Empire State Building completed in New York in 1931.
4. Orion's belt.
5. The Sphinx.
6. Nicholas Hagger, *Awakening to the Light*, p.36, 8 June 1963: "I wrote *The Great Pyramid* first version quickly because a lodger was coming to take over my room at 6. I wrote it between 4.30 and 6. Then the lodger decided not to come. Now for the second version at 7.30."

2

The Meaning and Purpose of the Great Pyramid

I

I can hardly contain my excitement. I have just had the most thrilling news. I have actually met someone from the Pyramid Committee who personally read my questions about the mystery of the Great Pyramid which I submitted nearly eleven years ago. I met him by accident, of course, for such an important meeting could not happen by design.

I had just finished work for the day and I looked in on a reception to mark thirty years' service on the part of one of the building managers. I had half wondered if Prince Hemiunu would be there, but he wasn't. As I entered, an attendant took me to one side and said, "You may like to meet our guest of honour, who's from the Pyramid Committee. He's in that room. Follow me."

I couldn't believe my luck. Quivering with excitement I followed the attendant through to a cool room where a distinguished-looking man with a noble face and upright bearing stood, holding a drink in a pottery wine-cup. He looked like an official, he had great presence, and immediately put me at my ease. "I saw your name on the guest list when I arrived. You wrote to the Pyramid Committee some while back?"

I nodded, a bit tongue-tied before such an important man and noting that he had identified me and presumably asked the attendant to introduce me to him as soon as I arrived.

"I remember your papyrus letter. The reply was delegated to one of our scribes, but I particularly remember your main question. It's one that I've often asked myself, what the purpose of this vast building is. But as you have yourself done such excellent service on the Great Pyramid, I can let you into a secret." He lowered his voice and looked around to make sure he was not being overheard. "I'm sorry to be the bearer of bad tidings, but I can tell you, in confidence, that Khufu is dead."

"Dead?" I gasped.

He nodded. "Exactly when he died I don't know, but I believe he's been dead some while. News of his death was hushed up so that the transfer of power could happen smoothly. The pyramid-workers do not know, but as you are an official with an important position I feel I owe it to you to tell you. At one time his successor was supposed to have been his oldest son Kawab, but as all know, he was unfortunately killed in tragic circumstances. It's his son Djedef who's succeeded him. He has taken the name of Ra and will subordinate himself to Ra. He will build his pyramid away from Giza, I'm not sure where."

I was still reeling at the momentous news of Khufu's demise.

"So where has Khufu been buried?" I eventually asked.

"I don't know. No one on the Pyramid Committee knows. Not here. Perhaps in a *mastaba*, near his mortuary temple," he conjectured. "He could not be buried in the Upper Chamber of the Great Pyramid."

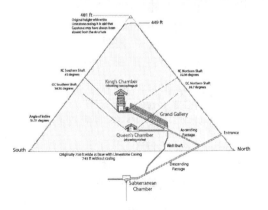

The Great Pyramid and the great gallery (Grand Gallery) of internal steps, and a diagram of its location in the Great Pyramid

I had suspected as much as his sarcophagus is standing empty in the Upper Chamber. Ever since I climbed the ramp between the high corbelled walls of the great gallery of the Great Pyramid under the guise of looking for one of my workers, and saw the red-granite sarcophagus being dragged in place and the walls and ceiling being built round it, I suspected this. For first the sarcophagus is wider than the entrance to the chamber, and all I have asked have denied that the entrance was subsequently made smaller. Secondly, Khufu's body must be dragged in the sarcophagus through wailing crowds to its final resting-place. But the red-granite sarcophagus could not possibly have been dragged up the steep incline to its final place – even if the entrance had been wide enough to take it; it could only have been placed there in the course of the building. And there are three chambers – one leading downwards underground and two above ground, one of which (the Upper Chamber) has five rooms above it. I myself have seen the inscription on the wall of the highest room: "Wonderful is the White Crown of Khufu", referring of course to the Upper Kingdom and not the Lower Kingdom, which is represented by a Red Crown.

"Even in Khufu's lifetime the decision was taken not to use the Great Pyramid as a tomb," the noble official told me. "One day there was a dreadful ear-splitting groan from the massive ceiling blocks of the Upper Chamber, each weighing between 3.5m and 6.6m debens,[1] and a great crack appeared. The noise was heard by many of the construction workers, who rushed in to see what had happened. It was felt that the Pyramid might be unsafe – that it might come crashing down – and the decision was taken within twenty-four hours by the Pyramid Committee that Khufu, whose face will stare from the great lion-shape[2] at the eastern horizon for ever, should not be interred in a monument that could collapse, leaving it open prey for tomb-robbers."

I was staggered. After so much planning and care, it was inconceivable that the Great Pyramid could have cracked up and that it had to be abandoned. There must have been dreadful consequences for such an obvious error.

The Great Pyramid

"What happened to those whose calculations did not anticipate this cracking?" I asked. "Who was accountable? Were officials blamed? What happened to them? Were there executions?"

"Oh no," he said. "This work defies the forces of nature, it's the biggest project the world has ever known. The miracle is that such size and grandeur is possible, not that cracks appear in it. Besides, the calculations were approved – not done, mark you, but approved – by none other than the vizier Prince Hemiunu and his chief architect Mirabu, and they – although I have never seen them, you understand – are in Khufu's court. No, nothing happened to anybody. That is not to say that errors were not noticed and noted, and have not been written by scribes on their records. Promotions may well be blocked as a result of that episode. I am not saying blame was not allocated. Only time will tell as the consequences slowly unfold. For round the Great Pyramid, as you well know, there is a culture of precision, meticulousness, accuracy, and nothing untoward can happen without grave consequences at a future date. And I can tell you...." He dropped his voice confidentially. "Despite what I have just said – which, you understand, is the official line – some officials were rounded up and incarcerated on the forbidden western side of the Great Pyramid where even you are not allowed to go, and they are.... Not mistreated, for they have deserved their treatment. Punished, that is the word. They are punished every minute of every hour of every day, in ways which are too dreadful even to bring to mind. But if you are asked, you now know the official line."

So it's astonishing. All this planning and organising and building for twenty-nine years and putting-on of the casing blocks so the whole Pyramid shines in the morning sun of Khepri, the midday sun of Ra and the evening sun of Atum – and the project has been so badly bungled that the Pyramid can no longer be used for the purpose for which it was built. And no one knows where Khufu's mummified body rests. Perhaps this is on security grounds, to keep it safe from tomb-robbers.

"So that's why the subterranean burial chamber is unfinished," I said.

"Yes, the two upper chambers had been more or less finished. Work stopped straightaway, nothing more was done in the subterranean chamber. The idea that Khufu would be buried in the Great Pyramid was abandoned, but the Great Pyramid had to be completed because Khufu wanted it. In fact, there was a problem because of the cracking. It was hard to persuade some of the working teams to continue. I can tell you now he's dead, but his daughter visited each member of the Pyramid Committee to plead with us to push the work on and compel the gangs to get it finished. She actually – seriously – prostituted herself among some members of the Pyramid Committee – not me, of course – to persuade them to continue the work. She offered her 'services' to anyone who would take the decision to push the work along. Khufu was still alive, and her prostituting herself was apparently done with his knowledge and blessing. Some members took her up on her offer with great enthusiasm and complied with her wishes. Of course, they paid lip service to the religious gloss put on her actions, that she was embodying the divine god and spreading his gift of immortality to the Pyramid Committee. But that is how the Great Pyramid is so near completion."

The news about Khufu's daughter was immensely shocking and incredible. I still can't believe it. That she should have offered herself to members of the Pyramid Committee with Khufu's knowledge.... I am dumbfounded. The great Khufu's daughter – Pharaoh's daughter, the daughter of a god – a prostitute! It is too dreadful to contemplate.

I did not know what to say. My mind was reeling. In all my calculations I had never dared to think that the great Khufu could be so self-serving and ruthless towards his own daughter, so corrupt.

"So why," I asked at length, "if the decision had already been taken to abandon this Great Pyramid as a tomb, did Khufu set such importance on completing the work, subjecting his daughter to such humiliation?"

The stone lion

"Because he was a god," my informant said simply, clutching his clay wine-flagon. "Here in Giza there was a local divine cult of Khufu, as we all know. Khufu did not take the name Ra because he had replaced Ra. It wasn't Ra who illumined Khufu's *akh* (his spiritual soul so he was a Shining One). Khufu himself received the power that illumined him, he was the *akh* that illumined our *akh*s. That's why that stone lion's been built...."

I thought of the massive stone lion that had gone up in recent times out of superfluous blocks that were not needed now the Great Pyramid was nearing completion. I had often wondered what it represented.

"The lion has Khufu's face looking calmly at the eastern rising of Khepri, the morning sun, and also Ra at midday and Atum, the evening sun. The lion is associated with mountains and the rising of the Sun-god. Khufu, '*Khut*', 'Glory', is looking towards the east, and even the rising sun Khepri and the midday sun Ra acknowledge his glory as being above theirs. The stone lion represents the deification of Khufu. Khufu is the *akh*, and our *akh*s shine from his."

Again I was reeling. So the stone lion's face *is* Khufu's. No one was sure of that. Khufu forbad statues of himself, and there are no images of him except illegal ones, like one only a finger's height[3] and wearing the crown of Lower Egypt which was shown to me when I visited the Temple at Abydos.[4]

"And the Great Pyramid?" I asked. "How does that fit in with Khufu's deification?"

"The Great Pyramid is covered in polished limestone casing stones to symbolise the *akh*. The whole thing is a temple to the *akh*, and living people wearing masks can go into the chambers and act out scenes about becoming an *akh*. That is the secret the priests keep, the re-enactment of rituals involving becoming an *akh* which guarantees eternity and an immortal life in the Eternal Sunshine."

I tried to make sense of what he had told me. "The answer I had from the Pyramid Committee was: 'Man needs the Great Pyramid.'"

"The answer you received was of course the interpretation of one particular scribe and has the status of one man's opinion. It was not the view of the Pyramid Committee, who were naturally informed of the reply. For nothing goes out from their offices without all members of the Pyramid Committee being apprised of every word that is being said. Nevertheless, the scribe was right. Man needs guidance to become an *akh* so he can follow Khufu into the Eternal Sunshine. Khufu has been saying, 'Work for me, build my pyramid, and you can be with me in the afterlife.'"

I was stunned. So ever since the cracking of the stone in the Upper Chamber, the Great Pyramid had been a cenotaph, an empty tomb – and a temple for rituals about becoming an *akh*. That is what I had spent nearly thirty years of my life pondering.

"How did you learn that?" I asked. "Who was your source? Khufu himself?"

"Oh no. No one on the Pyramid Committee has ever seen, let alone spoken to Khufu. We don't live in Memphis. I'm not at liberty to say where we live but like you we receive our instructions from a higher authority."

That in itself was a stunning new idea, that the Pyramid Committee is itself under another authority in the chain of command.

"No, this came from one of the Pyramid Committee who asked Khufu's daughter why it was so important to finish the building of the Great Pyramid. That is what she is reported to have replied. I believe the story, but I do agree, it's not a very good source."

"How many of you are there on the Pyramid Committee?" I asked. "I've heard some say, nine."

"It's more than that," he smiled.

"Three hundred? I've heard some say three hundred. As many as that?"

"Oh, I'm afraid I'm not allowed to disclose that. It's privileged information."

"Can I become a member of the Pyramid Committee?"

At that moment the attendant returned and said, before my informant could answer, that the construction workers awaited him, and now I stood back and bowed to allow him to be led to the reception. I followed holding my clay flagon of wine and stood at the back of a crowded room, and I did not manage to speak to my informant again. I listened to his few words of faint praise for the worker being honoured – my informant clearly did not know him – and turned to speak to another worker who approached me with a question about his compound; and when I looked back the member of the Pyramid Committee, my informant, had completely vanished. I could not find anyone who even knew his name.

II

So now my mind is racing. After nearly thirty years, do I at last have all the answers?

First of all, do I believe what I have been told? Was my Pyramid Committee member a reliable source? And was his source, Khufu's daughter, reliable? And had any member of the Pyramid Committee actually met Khufu's daughter, as he had said? And why had he volunteered so much information about the meaning and purpose of the Great Pyramid when he wouldn't tell me the number of the Pyramid Committee, which to me was far less important than the State secrets he revealed about Khufu's death, Djedef's succession, Khufu's daughter's prostituting herself on Khufu's instructions – I still cannot get my head round that idea – and the function of the Great Pyramid, that it is an empty *akh*, a blaze of Light. Now it has casing blocks on most of it, which reflects the sun, I can see the logic of what he told me.

In all my searches for a rational explanation over nearly thirty years, I overlooked the possibility that the Great Pyramid was an *akh* for ritual re-enactments by priests wearing masks of gods. So why the blocked air-channels? To absorb some of the candle-smoke – torch-light – these rituals might generate? Are they lighting aids, with deep vents so that those taking part in the rituals do not suffocate? And yet surely the channels, which are blocked with stops of a little finger's length[5] – as I've been told by one of the construction workers – cannot help the ventilation or flow of air for the living in the Upper Chamber with the red-granite sarcophagus?

I keep thinking again and again, man needs the Great Pyramid to become an *akh* and join Khufu in the Eternal Sunshine. I know that the true Ra is supposed to be an inner power all can find behind their closed eyes, although this is supposed to be given by the high priest of Ra as an intermediary and cannot be known directly without the hierarchy. Khufu himself is the Shining Ra, and his Great Pyramid, now it's encased, shines in the morning sun to his glory as the casing reflects the sun's rays. It is aglow in the morning and every sunset; on whatever side the sun is, it reflects and shines.

Yet when Khufu set out to build the Great Pyramid he did not have it in his mind that it would be an *akh*. Had the ceiling of the Upper Chamber not cracked, that room might have been his tomb – that is the implication of what the member of the Pyramid Committee told me. Or would Khufu have been buried in the unfinished underground chamber and not above ground? I think again, why does man need the Great Pyramid?

Furthermore, when he decided not to be buried in the Great

Pyramid, we are asked to believe, Khufu offered all men a chance to share his immortality. But until the ceiling cracked there was no plan to share it. He would have been buried there, I repeat, and the entrance to his tomb would have been sealed. So of how much value is a ritual that was a kind of after-thought, after the chance and arbitrary cracking of the Upper Chamber ceiling, not – never – a part of the meticulous plan for this operation?

The more I have thought about my meeting with my informant, the more I have begun to wonder if it was a blind. The attendant showed me into a private room. The member of the Pyramid Committee had seen my name on the guest list. Perhaps the whole story was an elaborate concoction to put me off the scent, following my letter? Perhaps Khufu is not dead, perhaps Djedef is not the present Pharaoh. And – I think this is quite likely as it is so shocking and unbelievable – perhaps the news of Khufu's daughter prostituting herself is a complete fabrication, a plant to lure me into repeating it so I can be arrested for sedition. Why, if Khufu is still alive and the Great Pyramid is his tomb, the story that it's an empty *akh* is itself seditious. Perhaps the approach to me was an instance of sinister Pyramid-Committee misinformation? Perhaps it is planned that I should be exiled for my question? Can my informant be relied on?

I now think I will be well advised not to repeat what he told me, for my own safety. On reflection, I think I will be well advised to forget everything I was told as it is too dangerous to share the news, given the organisation that has gone into producing a society round the Great Pyramid whose beliefs are so different from what the member of the Pyramid Committee told me.

And so now my excitement has cooled and I am aware that I am at odds with all those I have worked with for nearly thirty years. I know more than is good for me. And yet what I know is essentially without evidence or proof; it is at the level of a leak from the Pyramid Committee, which is extremely difficult to verify. If I were rash enough to ask any of my fellow workers on this project, "Is it true Khufu has died?" I would be reported immediately for questioning the basis of our long presence here – which is that we are doing Khufu's will and serving him, which is an honour seeing that he is a god.

Privately I have always doubted that Khufu was a god. If I were to say to one of my colleagues, "Khufu's dead and so we don't have to pretend to believe he was a god any more," and if it turned out that Khufu is still alive, I might disappear for ever.

So if I keep quiet about the revelation I received today, what do I privately think of it? I am being asked to believe that Khufu believed that the purpose of life is to become an *akh*, a Shining One, that can dwell with him in the Eternal Sunshine. If the purpose of life is to become an *akh*, I can see when you are *not* an *akh* the Great Pyramid may seem to have no purpose; whereas when you *are* an *akh*, the Great Pyramid may seem to have a purpose. The purpose of the Great Pyramid depends on one's perception. I can see that one's perception may reflect the level of truth one is at. And so, before one becomes an *akh*, the Great Pyramid may appear futile. But after one has become an *akh*, the Great Pyramid may seem to be a House of Eternity.

But I must stress, all this is theoretical. For I am not sure that I have been told the truth and I exercise some private scepticism about what I should believe. Should I be a fan of the Great Pyramid and an enthusiastic supporter of Khufu? Have the Pyramid Committee all become *akhs*, are they illumined Shining Ones? Is everyone on the Pyramid Committee illuminated? And when an official becomes an *akh*, does he still manipulate those below him? Is *akh*-hood a measure of inner saintliness or a kind of club which the Pyramid Committee join, which allows exclusive access to secret knowledge and which they use to outmanoeuvre or even destroy those slaves below them who do their bidding for nearly thirty years?

And so now I am even more confused than before. I have been told the answer to the question that has haunted me for nearly thirty years, but only a part of myself believes the answer. The rest of me – the majority of me – is incredulous, even sceptical. I need to consult a priest; preferably a high priest. Yet the very act of discussing what I have been told with a religious official could – if he reported me (as priests and high priests are known to do) – land me with a charge of sedition.

And so I have decided that I am neither going to believe nor disbelieve what the member of the Pyramid Committee told me. I will act quietly on the assumption that it is true, and will try to progress my becoming an *akh*, just in case what I was told is right. But I will not attach any great significance to my progress to *akh*-hood in case I have been told wrong, so I can avoid a trap that might have been set for me. In short, I shall continue as if I had not been told the answer to the question I asked nearly eleven years ago.

And in the evening, as I look up at the towering Great Pyramid that glints in the evening sun and throws its shadow towards the massive stone lion with Khufu's face, I shall think, as I take my evening drink, that it may be a tomb that towers over all and that it may also be a hollow sham; that it may be a temple for rituals about *akh*-hood and that it may also be an abandoned consequence of a bungle; that it may be a gateway – the gateway – to immortal life thanks to Khufu's questing knowledge and profound humanitarian feelings for his subjects, and that it may also be a botched job with ceiling stones that have cracked under the massive weight they bear, excused with tales of religious significance that may be no more than public-relations spin. I shall at one and the same time admire the meticulous calculations of the mathematicians which have raised this monument, the highest in the world, and deride the failure which omitted to take account of the weight the ceiling stones bear, which got wrong the durability of load-bearing stones.

And then I shall look above it at the vast sky which is also a tomb over all of us who are alive such a short while, and down at the sand that will cover us. I shall look up at the sun which warms my cheeks and burns my back, and I shall imagine I am an *akh* of Light in Eternal Sunshine which is always temperate, balmy and pleasant, and that all my uncertainties and doubts and rational questionings have been put aside as surely as if I had spread a cloth on the hot sand and laid myself out, closed my eyes and given myself to the warm, life-giving sun. I used to think that the sky, like the Great Pyramid, had no meaning or purpose in itself, but only what humans invested in it. But now I shall look at the sky and the temporal sun and invest them with a possible meaning and purpose – that they are scenery for my growth to an *akh* which will take me from this copy of a temporal sun to a greater reality, Eternal Sunshine; a meaning and purpose I have not been aware of until my chance meeting today. And I shall think this without reference to Khufu. And although everyone continues to praise Khufu's humane qualities, I shall think, privately, that he was in fact a tyrant who was in effect saying to us, "Work for me and be with me in Paradise" – and I shall say quietly, to myself: "I prefer the Paradise I consider when I am alone, after I have finished work and wander off and perceive through my *akh* and become one with the desert sand and sky and with sunshine that is both temporal and eternal."

8, 16, 20 February 2005[6]

Editor's Note and Footnotes

Diodorus Siculus maintained that Khufu was not buried in the Great Pyramid. Herodotus tells the story of Khufu's daughter prostituting herself to get the building of the Great Pyramid finished. Prince Hemiunu, the vizier, was Snefru's grandson and the building manager entrusted by Khufu with the building of the Great Pyramid.

1. In fact, 50–80m tonnes. During the Old Kingdom 1 *deben* was 12 to 14 grams. At 12 grams per *deben* 50 tonnes, i.e. 50m grams, equals 4,166,666.60 *deben*s; at 14 grams per *deben* 50 tonnes, i.e. 50m grams, equals 3,571,428.5 *deben*s. At 12 grams per *deben* 80 tonnes, i.e. 80m grams, equals 6,666,666.60 *deben*s; at 14 grams per *deben* 80 tonnes, i.e. 80m grams, equals 5,714,285.70 *deben*s.
2. The Sphinx.
3. "A finger's height", i.e. 7.5 cms.
4. Abydos had a temple from Khufu's time. Now it is occupied by a later temple which contains *bas*-reliefs carved in the reign of Seti I.
5. "A little finger's length", i.e. 7 cms or less.
6. Nicholas Hagger, *Diaries*, 8 February 2005: "In the *café* area [of Cairo airport] in front of Gate 3, extreme left front table, facing the gate, I scribbled the first two pages of 'The Solution to the Mystery of the Great Pyramid', the sequel (42 years later) to 'The Riddle of the Great Pyramid', and also had the idea for a project, Letters from Ancient Egypt, in which 7 papyri are discovered, including

'Riddle'.... A good flight and a long flying around over Heathrow (1 hour) – which allowed me to complete my revisions of 'The Riddle of the Great Pyramid'." *Diaries*, 16 February 2005: "By 6 began the sequel to 'The Riddle of the Great Pyramid' and finished it by 8.30 when I was called for supper."

3

The Great Pyramid as a House of Eternity

I

I am 80 now and Khafra is Pharaoh. He is building his own Pyramid, and it is time to set down my last thoughts on the mystery and conundrum of the Great Pyramid. For today I have set eyes for the first time on the face of the lion on the mound of natural rock.

Until now the mound of natural rock has been cordoned off and its front has been out of sight of us who have spent our working lifetimes near the Great Pyramid, just as the western side of the Great Pyramid has been out of bounds to us. I was told during Khufu's time that the mound had been reshaped into a lion with a man's head, Khufu's. Even though a papyrus in Saqqara[1] states that the lion's head was built by Khufu, that was misinformation, one of the hazards of trying to make sense of all the building that has been happening. It now transpires that there was an intention, an ambition, that did not actually happen. Khufu began to shape the mound of natural rock, but the finishing of the face did not happen. Nothing happened in Djedefra's eight-year reign either.

Solar boat of Khufu

But Khafra has taken up the idea and has implemented it. He has shaped the lion's paws at the front, and elongated its back as the mound of natural rock gave a problem with the rear paws and tail. The scale of the body has been 1:22, but the head is now larger, 1:30. It is the face of a man with large eyes and ears, a nose and lips. It faces east and looks for the sunrise. Khafra is "the son of Ra" as Khufu never was – he was a god who replaced Ra – and the lion's face searches the horizon for Ra and is bathed in sunlight as the sun rises. Teams of stonemasons have been shaping this face.

But no one has said whose face the lion bears and I have just found out.

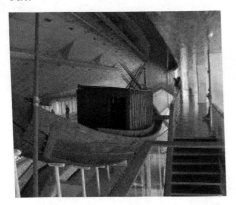

Another view of the solar boat of Khufu

Today something exceptional happened, which has never happened in all my years of building the Great Pyramid and burying Khufu's boats to take him to his second life. This morning I was approached, as a senior and trusted member of the administration in view of my years, by an important official in Khafra's team, and asked to take a papyrus message to the chief stonemason working on the lion.

I walked across the early-morning sand by the causeway in some trepidation, for it was rumoured that any found there who had not been given permission are put to death. I noticed that the causeway from Khafra's Mortuary Temple beside his Pyramid to his Valley Temple where he will be mummified skirts the mound of natural rock, indicating that the mound was there before the causeway was built. It was there in Khufu's time, so was the face of the lion?

I was directed to the stonemason, and found him up a ladder, standing on a strut fastened by bound ropes, working with a chisel and hammer on the lion's face. I looked hard at the face, at the ears, eyes, nose and lips, wondering if it was the face of a man or a woman. I looked at the alignment of the lion. It was perfectly in front of Khafra's rising Pyramid now, and is sideways-on in relation to Khufu's Great Pyramid. It 'belongs', from the point of view of perspective, to Khafra's Pyramid, not Khufu's.

The stonemason saw me holding up and waving the papyrus and came down the ladder with his hammer and chisel in one hand, and took my papyrus. He did not say a word, there were many others present and I had to act correctly. I bowed and withdrew when it was clear there was no message to take back, and returned across the sand to my side of Khufu's Great Pyramid.

But I had seen the face of the lion, and when I next had an opportunity, when I was asked to take a message to a stonemason in Khafra's Valley Temple, the Necropolis next to the lion for funerary rites where it is expected that Khafra's body will be mummified – now I am 80 I am deemed too old for hard work and am sometimes used to convey messages – I stopped near the entrance in the vestibule and looked hard at one of the black diorite statues of Khafra.

I was astounded. For the face on the statue has been replicated on the mound of natural rock that has been shaped into a lion. It is now clear to me that the lion's head is Khafra's, not Khufu's. The finger-long statue of Khufu (three inches long) I saw, which has Khufu's Horus name, Hor-Medjedu, inscribed on its throne, has different ears and thin lips, and is not the head on the lion.

I needed to confirm that the lion's head is Khafra's with the stonemason I had taken the message to, and I was fortunate. For as soon as I had returned to my base near the Great Pyramid the same official in the administration sought me out again with another papyrus, a new drawing, and asked me to take it back to the same stonemason up the ladder.

So I returned across the sand, in the heat of the day now, and stood again beneath the lion's head and waved a papyrus to attract the stonemason's attention, and he again climbed carefully down the ladder with his hammer and chisel in one hand, and took the papyrus. This time he was more friendly. He smiled at me. He was in his mid-thirties, I would say, and his face was burnished from working in the sunshine of Ra.

He stood and opened the papyrus in front of me and looked up at the face, working out a measurement that would affect his chiselling. And I felt emboldened to ask a question I would not have dared to ask when I was a younger man.

Life-size statue of Khafra in the Museum of Egyptian Antiquities, Cairo (right), and, for comparison, the face of the stone lion from the front, which looks identical

Close-ups of the faces of the Sphinx (left) and Khafra (right), showing a similarity in eyebrows, eyes (all four eyes have pupils), ears and lips. Khufu has ears close to his head (see pp.3 and 8).

I said casually, "You're shaping the face of the Pharaoh on the lion, are you not?"

He looked at me and corrected me: "The Pharaoh as the servant of the Sun-god Ra, yes."

"So that's the Pharaoh Khafra."

"Yes. Looking at the sun as it rises from the horizon to its zenith above."

Two images of Djedefra

I thanked him for answering my question and he turned back to climb the ladder and resume his chiselling. And I trod back over the burning sand excited and pleased that I had established that, although there was a plan to turn the mound of natural rock into a lion with Khufu's head, the lion's head was in fact Khafra's with a royal head-dress.

I found the official in the administration in his room and told him the stonemason would implement the drawing in his papyrus. He thanked me, and I said, "It must be a great responsibility to be designing the details of such an important head."

"Oh," he said, "the design is being done higher up by someone in the Pyramid Committee. Instructions come down to me and I have to make sure they are relayed to individual stonemasons. As you know, the Pyramid Committee began under Khufu and it adapted to the wishes of Djedefra, and it's adapted again to the wishes of our present Pharaoh, whose *ka* is the son of Ra."

I asked if he was involved in implementing the design of Khafra's Pyramid.

"Yes," he said, "I am involved in it."

Aware that he looked up to me because I am 80, judging him to be about 50, I said, "So far as you are aware, Khafra will be buried in his Pyramid, which you are helping to build?"

"There will be a burial chamber, that is all I know."

I said, "The Great Pyramid was built as a tomb but Khufu was never placed in it. So in a sense it's not a tomb at all."

He said, "It's the tomb of Eternity."

I was shocked. 'The tomb of Eternity', what did it mean?

He saw my incomprehension and said, "It's a tomb that is a gateway to Eternity, a gateway to the second life. It doesn't matter that Khufu is not buried in it. The triangular hieroglyphic in our formal language that looks like a pyramid means 'Eternity'. The pyramid tomb is a representation of Eternity, it resembles the sun's rays coming from a point at the top of the capstone down four walls to the north, east, south and west. To our present Pharaoh Khafra it embodies the rays of Ra, the Sun-god streaming downwards and guaranteeing Eternity, Eternal Light streaming down from one point in sloping rays like the walls of the Great Pyramid, and offering a gateway to a second life.

"But to Khufu, *he* was the sun, the god, and they were *his* rays. The Great Pyramid was called '*Akhet Khufu*', 'The Horizon of Khufu', because Khufu rose on the horizon at dawn and set on the horizon at sunset, and he was able to live between the east and west horizons here in the Great Pyramid, the House of Eternity. Viewed at a distance from the Great Pyramid, the sun sets *into* the Great Pyramid, which is his House of Eternity.

"So regardless of whether Khufu's mummified body was placed in the red-granite sarcophagus – and there are sound reasons as to why it wasn't, as the stone beams above the sarcophagus began to crack towards the end of the Great Pyramid's construction – his possessions could be placed under the downward rays of the sun and he could have been given a good send-off to his second life in Eternity, where he would be the main god.

"As I say, the Great Pyramid is an architectural symbol of Eternity within the sun's rays, it's the tomb of Eternity. It's where Khufu could take the large solar boat – that has brought blocks of stone casing [from Tura, ed.] and granite [from Aswan, ed.] to the base of the Great

Pyramid when the Nile floods and rises seven metres into the Basin of Khufu – to the second life where today we think Ra sails, and live where the sun goes for twelve hours of the night as the main god there."

I had not heard this before. For a moment I was speechless. Then I said, "So the Great Pyramid, which was built so carefully and with such mathematical precision for thirty years, is a space within the Eternity of the sun's rays that are angled down like the sloping sides of the Pyramid? It shows the way to the second life?"

"Yes," he said. "It lights up at dawn when the sun is on the limestone covering and in today's belief is lit by Ra, the Sun-god, on all sides. But Khufu replaced Ra, *he* was the god. He was deified, so the sun's rays were *his*. The Great Pyramid is within the Eternal Sunshine, it's a Hall of Eternity, a House of Eternity. And if Khufu was never buried in it, it still has a practical function. It creates inside it a space within Eternity surrounded by *his* rays, and will enable him to go to the second life where he will be the main god."

At that moment another official entered our room with a papyrus, and the official in the administration turned away from me, and I had to leave.

II

I walked away in a daze. I headed for a row of stone slabs and sat down in the warm sunshine and thought.

So all the organising for thirty years that I had given my life to, all the self-sacrifice of the teams of workers who like me lived on the site and devoted their lives to building the Great Pyramid, all the speculations as to what it meant while we worked without knowing why we were building it, all this came down to Khufu's personal conviction that *he* was the Supreme Sun-god and that he had to build a House of Eternity to embody the second life over which he would preside.

It was a preposterous idea. No man, even if he had been Pharaoh, can be the Supreme Sun-god. Khufu had been mistaken, he had been deluded about his own powers, he had succumbed to a gigantic folly, a foolish belief that was self-evidently nonsensical. He had been the top man in the country for the most important years of my life and he had been colossally wrong.

The Great Pyramid as a House of Eternity in the setting sun

His arrogance and self-glorification were mind-boggling. To believe what he believed was a sign of madness, insanity. And yet all his workers had trusted him and had faith in him. It was an outrageous situation. Now I saw I had given my life to building for a flawed man's self-aggrandisement. He had been egocentric.

Egyptians were supposed to subordinate themselves to the divine, whose presence priests approached in temples on their behalf. But Khufu *was* the divine, in his own mad mind he *was* the power behind the sun. He *was* Ra, he appeared to his people as the Supreme God. He should have been overthrown and sent into exile, run out of the country for sacrilege.

Then I realised, sitting in the sun, that Khafra had restored the

**The Sun-god Ra above Khafra's Pyramid
and the stone lion**

correct way of thinking. As the lion he sat calmly looking at the horizon for the dawn of the Sun-god Ra, who sent rays of light to light up his face. Khafra knew he was a recipient of the sun's energy, that it did not come from him. Khafra was wise compared with Khufu. He saw things truly, he subordinated himself before the divine.

I now saw Khufu's reign from the perspective of Khafra's. Khafra was the "son of Ra", a tradition that would last for over a millennium. His Pyramid, like Khufu's, had the entrance corridor on the north face to be orientated towards the circumpolar stars which were regarded as "the imperishable ones". Egyptians wished to dwell among them in the next world. His tomb chamber, like his father Khufu's, faced west, towards the kingdom of the dead. His temple for his cult, like Khufu's, was on the east side of the Pyramid, where the sun rose. His Pyramid still represented the primeval hill rising from the waters of the beginning as in traditional lore (as in the case of earlier *tumuli* and *mastabas*, rectangular flat-topped tombs on unbaked or baked brick). The tip of his Pyramid was gilded, like Khufu's, as it represented the sun from which rays of light shone down the sides and angles of the pyramid, and will envelop his mummified body.

Khafra, when buried, will enter into the celestial beyond as the son of Ra. He *will* sail to the celestial beyond in a solar boat. He, like Khufu, has a satellite pyramid for his *ka*. His *ka* will accompany him throughout his life as a kind of double, like his shadow, as did Khufu's, and will live on when he dies. It will leave its mortal house, the Pyramid, and return to its divine origin. All this is correct and as it should be.

Khufu, on the other hand, had all the outside traditional symbols and pointers to the second life but he corrupted the Egyptian view of Eternity by proclaiming himself the Eternal God who ruled the second life just as he ruled the first. He was above all humankind and Creation, and demanded to be worshipped while not encouraging human images to be made of him so he could be the Supreme God without an image.

I now saw clearly what my Great Pyramid should have been: a House of Eternity that would help Khufu to reach the second life. But I also saw clearly what the Great Pyramid was: a House of Eternity for Khufu, where Khufu could visit and dwell as the Supreme God when he came back to earth. I saw that Khufu would not have submitted himself to the judgement of Osiris after his death, but would be the Judge, the being of Ra and all the gods whose power he would harvest for his own use and gain.

I thought of Khafra's black diorite polished statue I had seen. The hawk-god Horus is spreading his wings protectively round the Pharaoh's head, expressing the connection between his earthly and divine power. Khafra was a man who fought to be energised by the divine power of the sun, and Horus the hawk was his link between the two.

Now I was indignant that I had given Khufu the best years of my life. I had worked punctiliously and had done everything I was told to advance the cause of the Great Pyramid. In the early days I had overseen the stone ramps with a series of post holes and supervised the putting-in of the thick wooden posts round which ropes were wrapped to create pulleys so teams could haul blocks up from below as well as from above.

I resented the many hard days I had spent grappling with how to raise difficult stones. At that time we calculated that if Khufu reigned 30 to 32 years the combined mass of over 95 million cubic feet [translated from Egyptian measurements of length] for his Pyramid, causeway, two temples, satellite pyramid, three queens' pyramids and officials' *mastabas* meant that his builders had to set in place 8,122 cubic feet of stone per day, at a rate of one average-size block, each weighing around 2.5 tons, every two or three minutes in a ten-hour day. And what was it all for?

All this phenomenal work of many teams toiling simultaneously through the heat of the day was to create a space where Khufu could proclaim himself the Supreme God, ruler of the stars and the sun, the embodiment of Eternity, living in a House of Eternity which would be his seat in this life as well as in the celestial beyond. And this was unbelievable and, worse still, plain wrong. For Khufu was a man, not a god. He would dwell with the gods and Ra by sailing in the boat, westwards with the setting sun and eastwards with the rising dawn, but he was not *the* Supreme God. His projection of his self into becoming ruler of the gods as Supreme God was sacrilegious.

Now I understood the tiny finger-sized image. He was such a powerful Supreme God that he banned all images of himself to live in the invisible, and if there had to be an image of himself it would modestly portray him in miniature. In reality the man was a tyrant. He had no feelings for his daughter, who he ordered to prostitute herself for his benefit, and he had no feelings for his subjects or his workers, who he treated as slaves. I had been a slave to Khufu's will, like all my fellow Egyptians who – when the Nile flooded and they could not work on their farms – did ten-hour shifts and lived near the Great Pyramid[2] and felt proud of our ranking in the hierarchy of the gigantic workforce.

We had all been brainwashed into thinking our activities were significant and worthy of the highest praise. He was an egotist who put his own reputation and power above all humans. I was right in what I had thought. The meaning of my life was not to work for Khufu's *akh* and assist his *ka*'s passage into the second life from his House of Eternity, but for me to work for *my akh* and assist *my ka*'s passage into the second life from *my* House of Eternity.

I had once met a tomb-robber. He told me, "When I rob a tomb I have to destroy the mummy so it won't tell on me in the second life and prevent me from going to Eternity." That's how I feel about

Khufu. I don't want him to spoil *my* chances of Eternity because I have rebelled against him. I have become a critic of governmental authority because it is self-interested and abusive, and I refuse to let Khufu prevent me from becoming an *akh* and my *ka* from going to Eternity.

And so I say to Khufu, "You are not the Supreme God. And when you have taken your place in the celestial beyond as an ordinary, humble man who has had his deeds weighed against a feather and been judged, you will not elevate yourself beyond the *ka*s of men like me who have as much right to enjoy the second life and Eternity as you have."

I say again, "I have as much right to Eternity as you, Khufu, and your swanky Pyramid can't elevate you above me and the rest of humankind. I don't care about your Eternity, I only care about *my own* Eternity. And I don't care about your House of Eternity. I only care about *my own* House of Eternity."

And so as of now I have retired. No longer will I run errands across the sand for a senior official in the administration. I don't want to look at the Great Pyramid, which has greeted me every morning for most of my life. I shall resign, give up my house to a younger worker, find a house with my savings and live simply near the Nile and work out my own salvation with diligence.

I will be disciplined and abstemious, I will speak to my *ka* as if it were my shadow and I will make something of my life. I will light up my soul and become an *akh* in the Eternal Sunshine. I will gaze at the rising sun across desert sand and love the temporal world, and I will turn my simple house into a House of Eternity, and when my time comes I will pass to the second life with my simple possessions and bask contentedly in the sunshine of the celestial beyond.

22–27,[3] 30 March 2020

Editor's Footnotes

1. Rolls of papyri (the oldest known papyri in the world) found by Pierre Tallet in 2013 in one of 30 sealed caves in a remote part of the Egyptian Desert a few miles from the Red Sea, a boat storage depot

during the Fourth Dynasty. One of the papyri, written by Merer, mentions Ankh-haf, Khufu's half-brother, as overseeing some of the construction of the Great Pyramid. Papyri have been discovered in the graves of the necropolis at Saqqara, and the papyrus suggesting that the lion-man the Greeks called the Sphinx was built in Khufu's reign was found c.2000.

2. Mark Lehner and Zahi Hawass, PBS, *NOVA*, 4 February 1997.

3. Nicholas Hagger, *Diaries*, 24 March 2020: "Started the resumption of the story for the solution to the riddle of the Great Pyramid: 'A Hall of Eternity.'"; *Diaries*, 27 March 2020: "Finished 'The Great Pyramid as a House of Eternity'. My hero turns against authority and cares only about *his* Eternity."; *Diaries*, 30 March 2020: "Dictated 'The Great Pyramid as a House of Eternity', which I finished about 4.30pm, and then walked."

Historical Notes

Historical Note on Khufu

Khufu ordained his Great Pyramid near the beginning of Egypt's Fourth Dynasty. An accurate timeline for his life is impossible as there is scholarly debate on the chronology of the Fourth Dynasty and the reigns of its Pharaohs. Papyri and stone inscriptions have been interpreted and reinterpreted by Egyptologists for more than 140 years. The evidence that gives a minimum length for Khufu's reign is an inscription on papyrus found in the port of Wadi al-Jarf, which describes royal boats in "the year after the 13th cattle count under Hor-Medjedu". It is generally assumed that cattle counts were every other year, and the length of Khufu's reign is to be found in the following alternatives:

- 23 years according to the Turin canon of kingship papyrus, 1,400 years after Khufu, suggested dates 2604–2581BC, or 2589–2566BC, or 2551–2528BC;
- 26 years if the cattle count mentioned in the Wadi al-Jarf papyrus was biennial, every other year, suggested dates 2609–2584BC;
- 32–33 years according to Rainer Stadelmann, see Appendix note 77 for source, and pp.xvi and 25–26 for his calculation that a limestone block in the Great Pyramid would have to be put in place every two or three minutes for his length of reign;
- 46 years if the Turin canon of kingship papyrus assumed that the cattle count was annual and not biennial;
- 50 years according to the Greek historian Herodotus; and
- 63 years according to the later Egyptian historian Manetho.

According to one view Khufu was born c.2620BC and came to the throne in his twenties. According to another view the Great Pyramid is thought to have been finished c.2560BC. But it must be stressed that there is no certainty in any of these dates as there are conflicting interpretations of the above six alternatives.

It can be said with some certainty that Khufu was preceded by Snefru (Horus name Nebma'at), and that he was succeeded by his son Djedefra (Horus name Kheper), who reigned for eight years. Djedefra was then succeeded by Khafra, also Khufu's son (Horus name Userib). Khufu's Horus name Medjedu can be found above the King's Chamber in the Great Pyramid, and also on the throne of the tiny three-inch ivory statue of him found in Abydos, which is now in the Museum of Egyptian Antiquities.

Historical Note on Khafra

Khafra (which means "appearing like Ra") was the son of Khufu, probably the younger brother of Djedefra, who preceded him. As with Khufu, there is scholarly debate as to the length of his reign, and the alternatives are:

- 24–25 years, evidence being the will of his son Prince Nekure that was carved on the walls of his *mastaba* and dated by a reference to the 12th biennial cattle count, and a reference to the "year of the 13th occurrence" on a casing stone in *Mastaba* G7650 suggested dates 2558–2532BC (assuming that Khufu died in 2566BC and Djedefra ruled for eight years after then – but if one of the other alternatives for Khufu's reign were true, that would give different dates for Khafra's reign); and
- 66 years, according to Manetho.

The face of Khafra is thought to be the face of the lion-man the Greeks called the Sphinx: (See the pictures on p.44.)

Appendix

The Egyptian Light

(from Nicholas Hagger's *The Light of Civilization*)

Like the Sumerians, the Egyptians symbolized the Central Asian shamanistic Light in their gods and State ceremonies, and numerous texts written on papyri and coffins invoke the Light and announce that their writers have become "Shining Ones".[1] As in Sumer and Akkad, the King – the Pharaoh – embodied the power and wisdom of the Light which was symbolised by the sun,[2] and the masses strove to become "Shining Ones" through a ritual that seems to have taken place in the Great Pyramid. This guaranteed survival after death, for the Egyptians interpreted the seeing of the Light as the gift of eternity, a guarantee of immortality in the Elysian Fields.[3]

Mesopotamian Origin and Cult of the Sun-God/Light

The Egyptian Light along with other aspects of the Egyptian civilisation may have originated in the Mesopotamian "Shining Ones".[4] Hieroglyphics may have developed from cuneiform, and Thor Heyerdahl's journeys show that the ziggurat could have been exported to Egypt and thence with the pyramid to South America. Some Egyptian religious cults may have originated in Sumeria.[5] The early African Egyptian society worshipped the African Ra (or Re) and (according to Frankfort's hypothesis) seems to have been influenced by Sumer.[6] Osiris, Isis and Horus may well have been Aryan-Sumerian gods, and there is an obvious parallel between Tammuz and Osiris, both of whom were associated with the Underworld.[7] About the time of the union between the Upper and Lower Kingdoms under Aha (or Menes) c.3100 or c.3032/2982BC,[8] Osiris became identified with Ra as we see from *The Book of the Dead*: "Osiris... goes into Tattu (i.e. Busiris) and finds there the soul of Ra; there the one god embraces the other, and become as one soul in two souls."[9] As Ra, the god ruled the Sky World and the visible world in his solar bark; as Osiris he ruled the

Underworld or the Kingdom of the Dead, and those who died with sanctity; and his son Horus (originally a falcon Sky-god) was the divine Spirit in every man on Earth.[10] To put it another way, Ra was the Infinite aspect of the Godhead, while Horus and Osiris represented God-in-man, first incarnate and then reunited with the Godhead after death. Egyptian religion was thus essentially monotheistic, the various gods being no more than forms, manifestations, phases, or attributes of the Sun-god Ra.[11]

This blending of gods with Ra led to a cult of the Sun-god. The belief that the King or Pharaoh was divine and that his soul blended with the Sun-god began c.2750BC, when the name Ra was taken by the second-dynasty Pharaohs Nebra and Neferkara. (The second dynasty began c.2853 or, on other datings, 2780 or 2770BC.)[12] It was well established by the fourth dynasty and intensified when the fifth dynasty associated with Heliopolis took possession of the Egyptian throne. It is referred to in *The Book of the Dead*: "I am Ra... when he began to rule that which he had made.... This means that Ra began to appear as a King."[13] From the early dynasties on, in his life, the Pharaoh was Ra and also Horus; on his death he was Osiris. He crossed the Lily lake to the East and once in the Underworld or Other World accompanied the Sun-god on his voyage out of the darkness and across the skies.[14] The morning sun was Khepri, the scarab beetle which pushed the sun across the sky; the midday sun was Ra; the evening sun was Atum.[15] Ra-Atum, the sun in its midday and evening manifestations, was pushed like a ball of dung by a scarab beetle (or dung beetle), or carried across the sky in a boat or on a falcon's wing, and according to the priests of Heliopolis could manifest as one of his offspring, Shu, the god of the air, which, in sunshine, meant sunny air.[16] When the moon-cult of the bull was taken over by the cult of the Sun-god, it was asserted that the sacred bull, Apis, was begotten by a ray of Ra's light.[17]

The fourth-dynasty Pharaohs who immediately followed Snefru and his son Khufu, who regarded himself as a god whom all should worship,[18] took the name Ra and identified themselves with the Sun-god. By the 6th dynasty (c.2347 or 2321BC), the Pharaoh was completely merged with the Sun-god;[19] he was actually the deity, and as the sun which made the crops grow was vital to the well-being of the nation, great care was taken with funeral rites to ensure that a dead Pharaoh actually became the god.[20] (It is now clear that the 3rd dynasty of Ur declared itself divine in the 22nd century BC as a result of Egyptian influence.)[21] At the beginning, only the Pharaoh-King was deified, only he derived magical powers from the sun, the "liquid of Ra" which entered his veins and enabled the Nile floods to appear on time and fertilise the soil.[22] The Pharaoh-King was the Sun-god, and when he died, his son was the Sun-god. Therefore the Pharaoh was reincarnated in his son, and some sort of transmigration from the father's soul into his son's soul must have taken place, via the sun.[23]

The Pharaoh's body, his *ka* (or life force), and his *ba* (his renown or impression made on others), interacted after his death, and he became an *akh* (or spiritual soul or spirit state, a glorified being of Light in the afterlife) which ascended to the stars (according to the Pyramid Texts), leaving a "Horus" or new living king behind him, and dwelt with the sun.[24] The *ba* is represented by the hieroglyph of the ibis; the *akh* is represented as a crested ibis.[25] It derives from the term for "radiant light", and the crest transforms the ibis bird of the *ba* into a "Shining One", an *akh*.[26] On death, the *ka* became a kind of double in which the life force could reside, and which required feeding.[27] At the beginning, only the Pharaoh had a *ka* or double and was reincarnated, but later, deification was extended to the royal family and a chosen few, and eventually it became a right to be claimed by all.[28] At first a dead physical body (*khat*) had to be mummified into a cocoon (like the pupa of a scarab) so that it would germinate or sprout a *sakhu* (*s'hw*) or "spiritual body" into which the *akh* ("glorious" or "shining one" or "spiritual soul") could pass.[29] Sir Wallis Budge in his 1899 edition of the *Book of the Dead* wrongly transcribed the *akh* as *khu*, but the hieroglyph for "spirit" or "spiritual soul" is clearly "*3h*" ("*a-kh*"), and Budge himself recanted in the 1920s and transcribed the Pharaoh "Akhenaton" correctly rather than as "Khu-enaton".[30] The *akh* in a *sakhu* dwelt in the Elysian Fields or Field of Reeds or Rushes which was the Egyptian Heaven after c.2000BC.[31] Later, mummification ensured that the *ka* would be born again in a counterpart of Egypt, in whose superior civilisation it would have the best chance of ultimately reaching eternity.[32]

*Akh*s or "Shining Ones" and *The Book of the Dead*

The widespread cult of the Sun-god did not merely pay honour to the exoteric sun; it also celebrated the esoteric Light. An experience of the Light in this life developed the *akh* and enabled the soul to survive in the Judgement Hall. This can be seen most clearly in the Egyptian *Book of the Dead*, which covers some 200 religious texts, spells and prayers in the form of revised texts (recensions) which were written on papyri or coffins between 1600 and 900BC, though many began as Pyramid texts and go back to 2400BC or before.[33] Traditionally these texts have been understood in terms of the afterlife, the references to Ra, Osiris and the sun applying to the Judgement of the Dead; and the title *Book of the Dead* – a mistranslation by the 19th century Lepsius which should really be translated "Chapters of Coming Forth by Day" or "The Book of the Great Awakening" (i.e. the manifestation of the Light)[34] – has been understood in terms of the coming forth into immortality after the first night in the Underworld.[35] It was a well-known Egyptian belief that a deceased spent the first night after his death journeying to the Underworld, and that he did not emerge into the realms of the blessed in Heaven until sunrise (*akhu*) the following morning,[36] when his hymn to Ra celebrated the survival of his soul, his "coming forth by day", which the texts, spells and prayers were designed to secure.[37]

However, the texts are at the same time to be understood in terms of this life, for the gods, who are all manifestations of one god, are all *akh*s,[38] which also means "glorious", "splendid" ones, "Shining Ones"; and the "Shining One", Amon-Ra (or Amun-Re), is the Light which brings eternity *now*. The hymns to Ra which open *The Book of the Dead* should therefore be interpreted spiritually as well as eschatologically. The illustrations in *The Book of the Dead* are of the rituals of living people, in which the high priest and priests put on masks of the various gods to act out roles in the story of Osiris.[39]

The Book of the Dead is thus a primer to help the *ka*, which was attached to terrestrial life and called the being to be born again, develop a *ba*, a supreme heart-soul or ghost that animated the body. This flew to its future abode as a human-headed hawk, as a stork with a flame, or as a "bennu bird" (or phoenix), the "eagle" of Herodotus which was probably a grey heron.[40] The *ba* could then become an *akh* or "Shining One" who was illumined. The *akh* was pure spirit, and was diametrically opposed to the mortal *khat*. *Akh* was the Pharaonic word for "light" in the sense of "glory" or "splendour" – the root meant "shine" or "irradiate", "radiant light"[41] – and as the Egyptians did not distinguish the eternal and temporal worlds in their hieroglyphics,[42] it could mean both physical and transcendental light, the Light of transfiguration and the uraeus (*akhet*) or cobra, the third eye.[43] The crested ibis which represented the *akh* was a migratory bird which lived on the Arabian side of the Red Sea and migrated to Abyssinia in the winter (a geographical equivalent for the spirit migrating to and from Heaven).[44] The glittering specks on the crested ibis's dark green plumage suggested its associations with the Light which was symbolized by the sun.[45] The *akh* preceded creation, and it was the aim of everyone to release it, shining, into the afterlife by activating it in this life;[46] for the Egyptians believed that the afterlife could be prepared for, and that a virtuous life on earth would increase the chances of the deceased when he stood before Osiris-Ra in the Judgement Hall.

Again and again, *The Book of the Dead* makes it clear that a virtuous life meant becoming an *akh*, seeing the Light. One of the oldest texts is Chapter 64, which occurs in two versions on an eleventh-dynasty coffin. The shorter version is called "Chapter of knowing the Chapters of Coming Forth by Day in a single Chapter" – in other words, it contained the whole of *The Book of the Dead* in essence – and its rubric attributes its discovery to the time of "Menthu-hetep" (clearly a mistake for "Men-kau-Ra", Mycerinus, of the fourth dynasty, the man who built the smallest of the three pyramids at Giza c.2539–2511 or 2490–2472BC) or even to the time of Semti or Den (or Dewen), c.2939–2892 or c.2875BC, although it may be much later. (See pp.69–70 .) The text proclaims: "I am Yesterday and Today; and I have the power to be born a second time. (I am) the divine hidden Soul..., the Possessor of two Divine Faces wherein his beams are seen. I am the Lord of those who are raised up from the dead, the Lord who comes forth out of darkness.... To the Mighty One has his Eye been given, and his face emits light when he illumines the earth. I shall not become corrupt, but I shall come into being in the form of the Lion-god; the blossoms of Shu shall be in me."

The blossoms of Shu are "the beams of the Sun-god" (Budge's note) – Shu (sunny air) being a child and manifestation of Ra-Atum – and they shall be "in me" (*im-i*), not "upon me" (*hr-i*). The rubric adds "If this chapter is known (by the deceased) he shall be victorious both upon earth and in the Underworld", that is, in this life as well as after his death. The Light shining "in" the writer brings success in this world and protection from evil in the Judgement Hall, and this passage contains what is perhaps the oldest recorded illumination from over 4,500 years ago.

The Book of the Dead charts an awakening – an initiation – from the world of the senses into the world of "the Shining Ones", in which the universe is filled with the "light of Ra". It is a body of advice to initiates whose illumination would stand them in good stead in the Judgement of the Dead. On their illumination they were received into "the sacred Heart of Ra".[47] According to the Hermetic literature of the 4th century BC, a man was released from earthly matter if a ray of Ra (or Amon) penetrated his soul,[48] a fact which resulted in many Egyptian names having something to do with the Light: Tut-ankh-Amon, for instance, meaning "Tut, the living image of Amon (i.e. the Light)" or "Tut who has life in Amon-Ra", the illumined Tut who will receive a favourable Judgement from Osiris. The "Chapter of Making the Transformation into the God who giveth Light in the Darkness" (80) is accompanied by a vignette (picture) of a god with the disc of the sun on his head, and the text is to be understood in terms of the living; indeed, the Egyptian idea of what happened to the dead was founded on their experience of the illumination that could be known by the living: "I am the girdle of the robe of the god Nu, which shines and sheds light upon that which belongs to his breast, which sends forth light into the darkness.... I have come to give light in (or lighten) the darkness, which is made light and bright (by me).... (I) have opened (the way), I am Hem-Nu (the Woman), I have made light the darkness,

I have come, having made an end of the darkness, which has become light indeed."

The illumined soul is like a lotus which grows from the neck and unfolds to the sun, like a flower opening to light, as the vignette for the first version of the "Chapter of Making the Transformation into a Lotus" (81A) makes clear. The second version of 81A, from the papyrus of Ani, shows a blue lotus in full bloom – the lotus being the symbol of the south (Upper Egypt), the papyrus being the symbol of the north (Lower Egypt) – and it can be translated in three different ways. First, "I am the pure lotus coming forth from the god of light (akhu), the guardian of the nostril of Ra, the guardian of the nose of Hathor. I make my journey, I run after him who is Horus. I am the pure one coming forth from the field." Or, "I am the pure lily coming forth from the Lily of Light. I am the source of illumination and the channel of the breath of immortal beauty. I bring the message, Horus accomplishes it." A more accurate translation interprets the hieroglyph akhu as "sunshine", in the sense of "Underworldly sunshine" (i.e. the Light): "I am this pure lotus which went forth from the sunshine, which is at the nose of Ra; I have descended that I may seek it (i.e. the sunshine) for Horus, for I am the pure one who issued from the fen."[49]

In the "Chapter of the Four Blazing Flames which are made for the Akh" (137A) the text states: "The flame comes to your Ka, o Osiris.... I cause it to come to (or, even) the Eye of Horus. It is set in order upon your brow.... The Eye of Horus... sends forth rays like Ra in the horizon." The Eye of Horus is the Light which is like the sun on the horizon, and the rubric says, "This shall confer power and might upon the Akh" and "these fires shall make the Akh as vigorous as Osiris".

The illumination is even more specific in the "Chapter of Kindling a Flame by Nebseni" (137B): "The white or shining Eye of Horus comes. The brilliant Eye of Horus comes. It comes in peace, it sends (or welcome, you who send) forth rays of light to (or like) Ra in the horizon." The movement from within to without recalls Coleridge's "I may not hope from outward forms to win/The passion and the life, whose fountains are within", and the tone becomes ecstatic and Zen-like: "The Eye of Horus lives, yes lives within the great hall; the Eye of Horus lives, yes lives." The joyfully illumined "Chapter of Making the

Transformation into a Living Soul" announces: "I am the divine Soul of Ra proceeding from the god Nu; that divine Soul which is God.... I am the lord of light."

Almost every page of *The Book of the Dead* is filled with the vision of the illumined "Shining Ones" (*akhs*), a vision which is reinforced by one of the hieroglyphs for *akhu*, or "Underworldly sunshine",[50] of a meditating god sitting and facing a bird, a crested ibis (his *akh* soul in his spiritual body or *sakhu*), which in turn faces a sun with three pyramid-shaped rays streaming down (the Light symbolised as the sun): "Behold, I have come forth on this day, and I have become an *Akh* (or a shining being)" (65B); "I am... the Great Illuminer who comes forth out of flame (or heat), the bestower (or harnesser) of years, the far extending One, the double Lion-god, and there has been given to me the journey of the god of splendour (*Akh*)" or "of a Shining One" (53); "I am Shu and I draw air from the presence of the god of Light (*Akh*)" (55); "I come forth to heaven and I sit myself down by the God of Light (*Akh*)" (74); and "I am one of those *Akhs* who dwell with the divine *Akh*, and I have made my form like his divine Form, when he comes forth.... I am a spiritual body (*sakhu*) and possess my soul... I, even I, am the *Akh* who dwells with the divine *Akh*" (78). "I, even I...." The ecstatic disbelief at a spiritual good fortune is caught with an amazing simplicity and directness that speaks straight to our hearts from the early Egyptian days.

The *Akh* as the Great Pyramid, Obelisks, Temple-Dancers

This obsession with becoming an *akh* or "Shining One" was at the heart of Egyptian life. The early phase of the cult of the Sun-god was behind the building of the pyramids, for although the tomb-pyramid began as a more elaborate version of the Kurgan long barrow with a deep shaft, first a *mastaba*, then a stepped, artificial mountain in a flat desert,[51] the pyramid form came to represent the rays of the sun bursting through cloud and shining down on the earth,[52] up which the king could mount to Heaven as an *akh*, as the Pyramid texts indicate: "I have trodden your rays as a ramp under my feet, on which I mount to... the brow of Ra."[53] There is thus a similarity between pyramids and ziggurats.

Khufu (more accurately Khnum Khofoy or Khnum-khuefi, "Khnum protects me"), the name of the Pharaoh who built the Great Pyramid (c.2604–2581 or c.2551–2528BC), was written *hwfw*.[54] The hieroglyph *hw* (*Khu*) can mean "Protector" but in this combination it is unknown and untranslatable – even such an authority as Faulkner omits it from his dictionary – and it is of a different root from *akh* (*3hw*) meaning "glorious", "splendid" or "shining". Nevertheless Khufu or Cheops (the Greek name known to Herodotus and used at the time of Alexander the Great) is associated with the noun *akhet*, the "horizon".[55] His Great Pyramid was called *akhet*, the horizon of Khufu.[56] *Akhet* also meant "radiant place". Khufu was described as being *akhty* (*3hty*) meaning "horizon-dweller"[57] (literally "belonging to the horizon" as "y" means "belonging to"), the hieroglyph for which includes two suns rising over horizons (one in this world and one in the Other World) and indicates that after death he would be a Shining being in the sunrise of the Light. Khufu, like his father Snefru, did not take the name Ra and is thought to have encouraged his people to believe in him as a Shining god. In consequence, a local divine cult of Khufu was established.[58] The Great Pyramid itself was called *akhty* ("horizon-dweller"),[59] i.e. "belonging to the horizon" – its full title was *Khufu akhty* ("Khufu, the one who belongs in the horizon") or *Akhet Khufu* ("the Horizon of *Khufu*") – and it literally shone like a Shining One for the polished limestone casing stones acted as mirrors and reflected great beams of light from one or other of the pyramid faces between sunrise and sunset.[60] The sides consequently shone gold in the sunlight – the Greek "pyramis" significantly comes in one of its derivations[61] from *pur*, "fire" – and it seems that the Greeks were reflecting the idea of "fire" in their word "pyramid". It seems that the Great Pyramid was built to embody the Light as Fire: its stones shone with divine Light (or Fire).

The Great Pyramid was the only one of the eighty pyramids built between the 27th and 18th centuries to have two chambers above ground, and there are four "air channels" from these chambers which could not have been intended for the *ka* (or double which lived on in the tomb and required food) for the *ka*'s life did not depend on physical air.[62] *Old Kingdom Pyramid Texts* (c.2345–2150BC) suggest that the *akh* flew (like a crested ibis) to the circumpolar stars, and a north-south section of the Great Pyramid [see diagram on p.28] shows that two of the "air channels" are inclined within an accuracy of one degree to the northern Alpha Draconis, the star round which turned the circumpolar stars that were "imperishable" (*Pyramid Texts* 1120–1123) as they never dropped below the horizon c.2550BC and therefore symbolised immortality;[63] and the other two to the southern stars of Orion.[64] It is possible that during the time of the Neolithic moon-cult the *akh* flew to the dark lunar Underworld, in which it survived like an immortal circumpolar star, but as the star-cult of the *Pyramid Texts* predates the sun-cult of the Pyramid-builders, which superseded it, it is certain that in the time of the Pyramid-builders the *akh* emerged into the pre-existent sunshine[65] (*3hw, akhu*) of the Heavenly horizon to "come forth by day" as "one who belongs to the horizon", i.e. a "horizon-dweller". Sun-worship of Ra took place during the second dynasty as we have seen, when Nebra and Neferkara took the name Ra. Nebra's reign was a good 200 years before Khufu's reign.

There is now a school of thought – most notably recently expressed by the authors of *The Orion Mystery* – that alignment with the stars was the predominant factor in Egyptian religious life and governed the building of the three Pyramids of Giza, which (to the Egyptians) represented the three stars in Orion's belt. However, so much is made of the *akh* in the time of the sun-cult and its rebirth to the sunrise, that the night sky could at that time only have been a symbol for the Underworld crossed by the *akh* before it was born in the sunrise of eternity. In short, certainly in the time of the sun-cult and possibly before, it was the sun, not the stars, that governed religious life and the building of the Pyramids. And the Great Pyramid may well have been sun-orientated rather than aligned with specific stars.[66]

In one of the many references to the *akh* in the *Pyramid Texts*, (*Pyramid Texts* 267–268) a Pharaoh is addressed in the Other World, "You are more *akh* than *akhu*", meaning, "You are even more pure spirit than the eternal pre-existent sunshine (i.e. the Light)".[67] The Great Pyramid must similarly be seen in relation to the *akh*. Quite simply, it *was* an *akh* – which is to say, it represented an *akh*.

There is a consensus that although the sarcophagi in the King's

Chamber and Queen's Chamber of the Great Pyramid are empty, they did contain the mummy of Khufu, Pharaoh of Upper and Lower Egypt, and his Queen; and that the mummies were stolen by tomb-robbers. But the "air shafts" could not have launched the soul into the Eternal Sunshine as they were bent and could not admit the sun and each was stopped up half way to the outer walls with two 8-cm-long stops. They were not even "air channels" which allowed living people to breathe.[68] Moreover Khufu may have died before the Great Pyramid was completed and may consequently have been buried in a *mastaba* elsewhere.[69] There is consequently a view that there was never any intention to bury Khufu in the Great Pyramid as the empty granite sarcophagus is too wide for the entrance to the King's Chamber, which shows no sign of having been narrowed. It can only have been dragged to its present place during the building, before the walls and roof of the King's Chamber were erected. The Great Pyramid was possibly therefore a cenotaph, an empty tomb, with one subterranean and two upper chambers, like Snefru's pyramid at Dahshur.[70]

It is possible that the above-ground sarcophagus in the King's Chamber was always an empty coffer, that the Queen's Chamber was for a statue of Khufu and that the underground chamber represented the Underworld.[71] Khufu's name appears on an internal wall of the top of five small chambers above the King's Chamber, as being responsible for building the Great Pyramid ("Wonderful is the White Crown of Khufu"),[72] not for being interred there – and it is possible that alone of the 80 pyramids with underground burials the Great Pyramid had an above-ground purpose.

According to a legend told by Diodorus Siculus,[73] Khufu was not buried in his pyramid. It is possible that this decision had much to do with the crack in the ceiling slabs of the King's Chamber, which may have appeared before the pyramid was finished and may have been accompanied by a terrifying noise that could be heard by all the workers. As a result the Great Pyramid may have been declared unsafe.[74] If this was the case, where was Khufu buried? Elsewhere in the Great Pyramid, in a hitherto undiscovered sealed room? Or in a hitherto undiscovered location? That is surely unlikely, given the huge amount of planning and effort that went into the Great Pyramid. If he died before the Great Pyramid was completed, he would have been buried in a *mastaba*, for no Pharaoh in his day could be buried in an uncompleted tomb.[75] The indications are that although he may have died before the subterranean tomb was completed – for it seems to have been left unfinished – the rest of the Great Pyramid *was* finished before he died. Scholarly opinion believes that he reigned longer than the 23 years stated in a Turin papyrus compiled 1,400 years later.[76] The papyrus gives suspiciously similar lengths for the reigns of Huni (24 years), Snefru (24 years) and Khufu (23 years), suggesting estimates of a generation on the throne. A reign of 30–32 years has been proposed.[77] The whole question of where Khufu was buried is a mystery.

It is possible that the Great Pyramid was a gigantic *akh*, a shining Khufuesque Cathedral where for more than two thousand years neophytes were initiated into the Mysteries of the *akh* by acting out the experience of illumination with high priests and priests wearing head-and-shoulder masks of the gods, playing parts in a Freemasonic-style initiation; just as later neophytes were initiated into the Mysteries of Isis. In this case the upper "burial" chambers were places of initiation rather than tombs, for a ritual whose texts are partly contained in *The Book of the Dead*. Marsham Adams was the first to connect the *Book of the Dead* and the Great Pyramid in texts like "This is a composition of exceedingly great mystery.... It is an admirable thing for everyone to know it; therefore hide it. Book of the Mistress of the Hidden Temple is its name" (rubric of ch 162); and "You have not gone dying, you have gone living to Osiris" (coffin of Amamu of Abydos). It has been suggested that the ritual involved passages and opening doors, and also (possibly) a rebuilding of the Great Pyramid (just as the Freemasonry ritual involves a rebuilding of the Temple).[78]

The initiate would have approached the Pyramid at sunset when it was a blaze of light from the evening sun (*atum*), and would literally have "entered the Light (or Fire)" (the horizon-Light of *Akhty*). He then underwent a ritual death in the down passage and ascended the first ascending passage to be reborn to Light among the air pockets of the upper chambers. He opened himself to illumination before the empty coffer (now missing but on record) in the Queen's Chamber,[79] and then followed the Path of the Just[80] up the ramp between the corbelled walls of the Grand Gallery to the ante-chamber and King's Chamber, where another empty coffer symbolised the empty tomb of the risen Osiris, the Hidden Light. There he became "a Shining One". The ritual took a whole night until dawn.[81]

The Great Pyramid was guarded outside by the Sphinx, who was called *Khu* (*hw*) or Protector.[82] There has been much speculation about the age of the Sphinx. It has been suggested that the Sphinx is 12,000 years old because of the amount of wind erosion – yet it was buried under sand for hundreds of years. Traditionally it was thought to have been created during Khafra's reign as it is linked to Khafra's pyramid by a causeway, and many books assert this.[83]

However, scholarly research suggests that it was in fact created during Khufu's reign as he was the originator in the fourth dynasty and his two sons who succeeded him followed his innovations: Djedefra (who took the name Ra and reigned nine years) and then Khafra (who also took the name Ra and built his own pyramid at Giza). Rainer Stadelmann of the German Archaeological Institute in Cairo, who organised the sending of a robot camera up the air channels and located the stops, holds this view;[84] he argues that wide-open eyes are more typical of Khufu's reign than of Khafra's; that the ears of the Sphinx are broad and folded forward whereas those of Khafra are elongated and closer to his forehead; and that the slanting causeway connecting Khafra's pyramid to the temples was built round the Sphinx, suggesting that the Sphinx was already in existence. A headstone from Khufu's time says, "Please make a way round (or to) the Sphinx," suggesting that the Sphinx was known in Khufu's time.[85]

If the Sphinx is Khufu looking at Ra in the east and being illumined by Ra's beams, he has an expression of supreme serenity and tranquillity – perhaps calming down the religious unheavals during his reign, when he had moved against the temple priests, declaring his own divinity.[86] The Sphinx may be saying: "Order has been restored by becoming an *akh*." If the Sphinx was built by either Djedefra (as has been suggested by the French Egyptologist Vassil Dobrev) or by Khafra, then the image is of their father Khufu, identifying him with the Sun-god Ra to restore respect for the dynasty after Khufu's religious persecutions.[87] Khufu is looking at Ra in the east and being illumined by Ra's beams, and his expression of serenity and tranquillity perhaps calms down the religious upheavals of his (i.e. Khufu's, their father's) reign, pledging that the Pharaoh now acknowledges the Sun-god and will not suppress the temple priests. In that case the Sphinx may say, "Order has been restored because we now become an *akh* through uniting with Ra." The Sphinx's riddle was that, looking to the east at the rising sun on the horizon, he was illumined with the peace of the Sun-god, the Light, and had become a Shining One, an *akh*, a "horizon-dweller". The true riddle of the serene and tranquil Sphinx was thus knowledge of the Light.

The Queen's Chamber and King's Chamber, then, may not have been tombs but may have represented successive stages in the mystic life as long ago as c.2550BC, and the *akh* was well known in the reign of Semti-Hesep-ti of the 1st dynasty (c.2875BC),[88] in whose reign (according to the rubric) the longer version of chapter 64 of *The Book of the Dead* ("The Chapter of Coming Forth by Day in the Underworld") was found; suggesting that this extract was written at a still earlier date: "My *akh* shall be as an amulet for my body and as one who watches to protect my soul and to defend it."

The Sphinx, the human-headed lion, then, may have represented Khufu, or possibly his son Khafra, as the Sun-god Khepri-Ra (or as Atum's child the "Lion-god" Shu, sunny air – or as Horemakht, "Horus on (or in) the horizon") whom he became after his death. This interpretation is confirmed by an inscription on the granite stela of Thutmose IV found in a royal chapel at the base of the Sphinx's chest. Thutmose called the Sphinx "this very great statue of Khepri", the god of the rising sun; and "Khepri-Ra-Atum", the Sun-god rising in the morning, at its zenith at midday and setting in the evening.[89] The Khufu- or Khafra-Sphinx guarded the necropolis at Giza (lions being regarded as guardians of the gates of the Underworld in Egypt).[90]

The cult of the Sun-god was also behind obelisks: according to Pliny, an obelisk "is a symbolic representation of the sun's rays and this is the meaning of the Egyptian name for it".[91] It combined the shaman's world axis (*Axis Mundi*), pillar or World Tree, with a ray of light, as did the spire, minaret and pinnacle of a church, mosque and Buddhist temple. Obelisks date from the 26th century BC, and the earliest surviving one (12th dynasty, 20th–18th centuries BC) stands outside the Temple of Amon-Ra at Karnak. The one undamaged obelisk from Heliopolis (c.1450BC) now stands beside the Thames as Cleopatra's Needle. The obelisks weighed between 140 and 230 tons, and their erection was a considerable mechanical feat.

Later, paintings in the tombs of old Thebes's west-bank Valley of the Kings (16th–11th centuries BC), which is across the Nile from Luxor, showed the angelic "Shining Ones" (*akhs* or "spiritual souls" which dwelt in their *sakhus* or "spiritual bodies") dancing. The temple-dancers of Luxor who lived in the annexe of the Temple at Karnak called the House of Life – the tombs in the Valley were called "Houses of Eternity" – represented the Shining Ones in eternal dances, and to do this they had to receive the Shining Ones, who were reflections of the Light of Ra, and raise their souls into the higher dimensions by *sekhem*, the divine power.[92] The temple-dancers in the Temple of Amon-Ra, Karnak (which was enlarged in the 15th century BC) therefore danced through their souls and became *akhs*.

Notes and References to Sources for The Egyptian Light

1. In their translations of the Egyptian *Book of the Dead* Sir E.A. Wallis Budge translates *"akh"* ("Shining One") as *"khu"*; R.O. Faulkner as "dweller in the sunshine"; and E.O. James as "glorified personality". When correctly translated, "Shining Ones" can be found on almost every page of *The Book of the Dead*.

2. For the Pharaoh as the physical sun of the Sun-god Ra, see E.O. James, *op. cit.*, pp.69, 108.

3. For the Egyptian belief in immortality in the Elysian Fields, see E.O. James, *op. cit.*, p.61.

4. Toby Wilkinson, *Genesis of the Pharaohs: Dramatic New Discoveries that Rewrite the Origins of Ancient Egypt*, claims to have discovered the origin of the Egyptian civilisation in the Eastern Desert, between the Nile Valley and the Red Sea, where there are rock drawings of hunters and herders and of flotillas of ships. The question is, did Wilkinson's expedition find the first Egyptians, or a desert culture

(c.4000BC) which the Egyptians absorbed? Samuel Noah Kramer wrote *History Begins at Sumer*. André Parrott in *Sumer: The Dawn of Art*: "Now that we can view the Mesopotamian Basin in all its splendour it is becoming clear that this flame which blazed up so suddenly in the Middle East, and shed so wide a light, was kindled at several points.... Susa, Lagash, Ur, Uruk, Ashnunnak, Assur, Nineveh, Mari – all alike were centres whose civilisation advanced from strength to strength until, at last, thanks to the genius of the few and the boldness of the many, there was wrought forth... a prodigious, many-sided art." Quoted in O'Brien, *The Megalithic Odyssey*, p.112. For "Mesopotamia-first" views, see *The World's Last Mysteries*, Reader's Digest, p.169 and *The Collins Atlas of World History*, pp.12–15. The Mesopotamian "Shining Ones" have their counterpart in Egyptian *akhs*.

5. *EB [Encyclopaedia Britannica]*, V.25. Heyerdahl's first voyage in 1947 on the *Kon-Tiki* was from the Pacific coast of South America to Polynesia to prove the possibility that the Polynesians may have originated in South America. His later voyages in 1969 from Morocco to within 600 miles of central America in a reconstructed Egyptian reed boat confirmed the possibility that pre-Columbian cultures may have originated in Egypt or been influenced by Egyptians. Budge, *The Book of the Dead (Theban Recension)*, p.xix: "If the known facts be examined it is difficult not to arrive at the conclusion that many of the *beliefs* found in *The Book of the Dead* were either voluntarily borrowed from some nation without, or were introduced into Egypt by some conquering immigrants who made their way into the country from Asia, either by way of the Red Sea or across the Arabian peninsula; that they were brought into Egypt by new-comers seems most probable."

6. For Ra as an African god native to On/Heliopolis/Egypt rather than an import from the East, see E.O. James, *op. cit.*, pp.71, 81 and elsewhere; E.A. Wallis Budge, *The Book of the Dead (Theban Recension)*, p.xxv: "It is easy to see that the debt which the indigenous peoples of Egypt owed to the new-comers from the East is very considerable, for they learned from them the art of working in metals... and the art of writing. M. de Morgan... thinks

that the art of brick-making was introduced into Egypt from Mesopotamia, where it was, as we learn from the ruins of early Sumerian cities, extensively practised, with many other things which he duly specifies." For Henri Frankfort's anthropological approach to archaeology and his *Kingship and the Gods*, see *EB*, IV. 281.

7. See E.O. James's notes on Frankfort in E.O. James, *op. cit.*, pp.347–349, 351.

8. For Menes as Aha, see Stephan Seidlmayer, 'The Rise of the State to the Second Dynasty' in *Egypt: The World of the Pharaohs*, pp.25, 27, 30ff, 33; and for the last dates see p.528 in the same book. See note 12 on double dating. *EB*, 6. 464 sees Aha as Menes' successor.

9. Chapter 17 of *The Book of the Dead*. The vignette illustrates both as hawks. Ra has a sun disc on his head, Osiris has a human head and wears a crown.

10. E.O. James, *op. cit.*, pp.31, 108.

11. Wallis Budge, *Egyptian Religion*, pp.13–15.

12. All Archaic-period and Old Kingdom Egyptian dates are approximate. The earlier date comes from Jürgen von Beckerath, *Chronologie des pharaonischen Ägypten*, MÄS 46, Mainz, 1997. The later dating is adopted by many books on Egypt and sanctioned by Zahi Hawass, Secretary General of the Supreme Council of Antiquities and Director of the Giza Pyramids excavations. The last date is based on the chronology developed by Prof. John Baines and Dr Jaromir Malek in their *Atlas of Ancient Egypt*. Where two dates are given in this section, they refer to the first and last schemes mentioned in this note.

13. *The Book of the Dead*, ch.17, quoted by Kurt Sethe, *Urkunden des aegyptischen Altertums*, vol VI. In E.O. James, *op. cit.*, pp.107/327.

14. E.O. James, *op. cit.*, pp.108, 174–175.

15. Mark Lehner, *The Complete Pyramids*, p.34.

16. Lehner, *op. cit.*, pp.23, 34.

17. Veronica Ions, *Egyptian Mythology*, p.122; Flavia Anderson, *op. cit.* Also *EB*, I. 445: "As Apis-Atum he was associated with the solar cult and was often represented with the sun disk between his horns."

18. Khufu did not take the name Ra, unlike his sons. That he regarded himself as a god is hinted at in many books and confirmed by the author's questioning of Egyptologists in Cairo. The norm may have been otherwise. E.O. James, *op. cit.*, p.116, quotes Moret (*Le Rituel du Culte Divin Journalier en Egypte*, Paris, 1902, pp.283ff) as contending that the Pharaoh was worshipped from the moment of his coronation, whereas Erman (*Handbook of Egyptian Religion*, London, 1907, pp.37ff) held that he was only formally worshipped with temples, offerings and priests after his death.

19. E.O. James, *op. cit.*, p.108.

20. For details of the coronation ceremony and toilet ceremonies, when the Pharaoh performed his renewal ritual every morning, see E.O. James, *op. cit.*, pp.111–114; E.O. James, *op. cit.*, pp.108ff.

21. *EB*, 18. 1021–1022; *EB*, 11. 973, 1005; E.O. James, *op. cit.*, p.65.

22. E.O. James, *op. cit.*, pp.115–116. Also see Flavia Anderson, *op. cit.*

23. For the divine succession by hereditary sequence from father to son, see E.O. James, *op. cit.*, pp.109ff.

24. Lehner, *op. cit.*, pp.23–24.

25. Lehner, *op. cit.*, pp.23–24.

26. Lehner, *op. cit.*, p.24.

27. Lehner, *op. cit.*, p.23.

28. James, *op. cit.*, pp.169, 261.

29. Budge, *op. cit.*, p.lxiv.

30. I am indebted to Carol Andrews, when she was Assistant Keeper in the Department of Egyptian Antiquities in the British Museum, London, for showing me pages from R.O. Faulkner's handwritten dictionary of hieroglyphs that clarify the various signs for *akh*, *akhu* and *akhty*, and for advice on a number of linguistic points in this section.

31. Budge, *op. cit.*, pp.lxvii, lxix.

32. Budge, *op. cit.*, p.lxxiii. Also, Miroslav Verner, *The Pyramids*, p.37: "Every Egyptian wanted to die in Egypt, to be buried there, and to be worshipped after death as an eternal memory."

33. Budge, *op. cit.*, p.v.

34. Lucie Lamy, *Egyptian Mysteries*, p.27. The full translation should be: "Book of the Coming Forth into Day, to Live After Death".

35. Budge, *The Book of the Dead (Theban Recension)*, p.lxxxviii: "The allusion being to the well-known belief of the ancient Egyptians that the journey to the Other World occupied the deceased the whole night of the day of his death, and that he did not emerge into the realms of the blessed until the following morning at sunrise."

36. But the whole burial ritual, including mummification, was generally expected to last 70 days, and sometimes took getting on for a year to complete – see Verner, *op. cit.*, p.36.

37. Budge, *op. cit.*, pp.3–17: hymn to Ra in papyri of Ani, Qenna, Hu-Nefer and Nekht.

38. See Budge, *Book of the Dead (Papyrus of Ani)*, pp.xci–xciii, on monotheism behind polytheism.

39. Lamy, *op. cit.*, pp.23–24, on initiation.

40. Lehner, *op. cit.*, pp.23–24. *EB*, X. 881.

41. Lehner, *op. cit.*, p.24.

42. Lamy, *op. cit.*, pp.24–25: "It is impossible not to relate this inner light to the Pharaonic word for light, *akh*. This word, often translated as 'transfigured', designates transcendental light as well as all aspects of physical light.... *Akh* indeed expresses all notions of light, both literally and figuratively, from the Light which comes forth from Darkness to the transcendental light of transfiguration."

43. Lamy, *op. cit.*, p.25.

44. The white ibis can still be seen round Luxor; drive by convoy – because of the military situation – from Luxor to Abydos and you will pass hundreds of ibises standing by the water of the roadside canals.

45. Lamy, *op. cit.*, pp.24–26.

46. Lamy, *op. cit.*, p.25.

47. Edith Schnapper, *The Inward Odyssey*, p.129.

48. Sir F. Petrie, *Personal Religion in Egypt Before Christianity*, p.49.

49. The first translation of 81A is, like the translations so far, from Sir E.A. Wallis Budge's *The Book of the Dead*. These translations are not always accurate. R.O. Faulkner's *The Ancient Egyptian Book of the Dead* is more accurate. It is from this book that the third translation of 81A is taken. The second translation of 81A is quoted in A.

Bothwell Gosse's *The Lily of Light*.

50. Lamy, *op. cit.*, p.25, which speaks of the "pre-existent *Akhw*" i.e. *Akhu* (as *w* is sounded *u*). Also see page reproduced in Hagger, *The Fire and the Stones* from R.O. Faulkner, *Concise Dictionary of Middle Egyptian*, which shows the hieroglyph for *Akhu*, which is defined as "sunlight, sunshine". As the *Akh* is "pre-existent", the sunshine is "pre-existent", i.e. underworldly.

51. Lehner, *op. cit.*, pp.14–16.

52. *The World's Last Mysteries*, Reader's Digest, p.190.

53. See I.S. Edwards, *The Pyramids of Egypt*, pp.290–291: Spell 508; and pp.139–140 for the Sphinx.

54. Ian Shaw and Paul Nicholson, *The British Museum Dictionary of Ancient Egypt*, p.152. Lehner, *op. cit.*, p.108. For the *cartouche* of Khufu's name (*hwfw*), see Alberto Siliotti, *Guide to the Pyramids of Egypt*, p.50, which shows a *cartouche* in red ink of Khufu, bearing his name and the year of his reign – "the seventeenth year of the (cattle) census". This was discovered on the walls of the highest weight-relief chamber by Vyse and Perring in 1837.

55. Lehner, *op. cit.*, p.108. Also Lehner, *op. cit.*, p.29: "In the Pyramid Texts, *Akhet* is written with the crested ibis and elliptical land-sign, not with the hieroglyph of the sun disk between two mountains that was used later to write 'horizon'." This also applies to note 56.

56. Lehner, *op. cit.*, pp.33, 108; Verner, *op. cit.*, p.189.

57. R.O. Faulkner, *Concise Dictionary of Middle Egyptian*, *Akhty* described as "horizon-dweller, especially of god" or "horizon-dwelling" – see note 50 for page reproduced in Hagger, *The Fire and the Stones*, showing *Akhty*.

58. Verner, *op. cit.*, p.236: "Recently Vasil Dobruv has suggested that Djedefra built the Sphinx as a gesture of filial piety connected with the establishment of the local divine cult of Khufu." Djedefra, Khufu's son and successor, was the first Pharaoh we know to take the title "Son of Ra". Khufu did not take the name "Son of Ra", and it is known that he persecuted temple priests. The indications are that he wanted himself to be worshipped as a god. The Sphinx may bear his face staring serenely at the sun, and the secret of the Sphinx may be: Khufu's divinity. If one of his sons was responsible

for the Sphinx, the statue could be intended to placate Khufu's people by reassuring them that his successor had subordinated himself to Ra.

59. Lehner, *op. cit.*, pp.108, 29.

60. Lehner, *op. cit.*, pp.108, 29, 6; Lamy, *op. cit.*, p.25.

61. For the derivation from *pur*, "fire", see Verner, *op. cit.*, p.460. "Pyramid" is also derived from the Greek for "wheaten cake"; see Lehner, *op. cit.*, p.460.

62. Lehner, *op. cit.*, p.23.

63. Lehner, *op. cit.*, pp.112–113; Verner, *op. cit.*, pp.202 and 41, 45: "After his death the ruler became one of the eternal stars near the North Star.... The dead pharaoh went north to become one of the eternal stars around the North Star that never set." Lamy, *op. cit.*, p.28: "In 2700BC, the Pole was occupied by Alpha Draconis, the star around which turned the Circumpolars – called the 'indestructibles' since they never disappear below the horizon. Thus they were the symbol of immortality."

64. Lehner, *op. cit.*, p.112; Verner, *op. cit.*, p.202.

65. Lehner, *op. cit.*, pp.28–29; Lamy, *op. cit.*, p.25. Verner, *op. cit.*, p.44: "The pharoah's ultimate goal was to rise as high as the sun that 'shone over the horizon.'"

66. See quotation in note 65.

67. Lamy, *op. cit.*, pp.25, 28.

68. Lehner, *op. cit.*, p.114.

69. Verner, *op. cit.*, p.203: "According to a legend recounted by Diodorus Siculus, Khufu ultimately was not buried in his pyramid. Medieval Arab historians mention the existence of a mummy-shaped coffin and the ruler's bodily remains but do not say where they lay."

70. Lehner, *op. cit.*, pp.99–100, 103.

71. Lehner, *op. cit.*, p.114. It was Rainer Stadelmann who suggested that the unfinished state of the subterranean chamber meant that it was intended to resemble the Underworld cavern.

72. For the *cartouche* of Khufu, see Siliotti, *op. cit.*, p.50. "Wonderful is the White Crown of Khufu" – reported to the author by an Egyptologist accompanying him inside the Great Pyramid.

73. Verner, *op. cit.*, p.203. See note 69.

74. Verner, *op. cit.*, pp.202–203. That the cracking in the ceiling of the King's Chamber made the Great Pyramid unsafe was first claimed by the Polish architect Koziński.

75. Knowing what we do about the respect and reverence for the Pharaoh, we can safely conclude that no Pharaoh could be submitted to the indignity of being buried in an unfinished tomb.

76. Lehner, *op. cit.*, pp.38, 108.

77. By Rainer Stadelmann, *Pyramiden*, L.A.IV, 1982, pp.1205–1263; and *Die ägyptischen Pyramiden: vom Ziegelbau zum Weltwunder*, Mainz, 1985.

78. See R.G. Torrens, *The Golden Dawn and the Inner Teachings*, pp.150–151, for treatment of the Great Pyramid as "Light" and an initiation into the mysteries of the *akh*.

79. Marsham Adams, *The House of the Hidden Places* and *The Book of the Master*, both published in 1895, suggested that the Great Pyramid was used for ceremonies of initiation; that the postulant goes through the symbolic ritual of *The Book of the Dead*, which is full of doors opening and closing, and finally lies in the tomb of Osiris, the Hidden Light. See Torrens, *op. cit.*, pp.11, 65, 150–152. Also see Verner, *op. cit.*, p.450.

80. There is no evidence that the ramp was originally called the Path of the Just; this may be a relatively modern label giving it a ceremonial purpose. Compare "King's Chamber", "Queen's Chamber" – which are relatively modern labels.

81. See note 79.

82. Manfred Lurker, *The Gods and Symbols of Ancient Egypt*, p.114: "The Egyptian sphinx was, with only a few exceptions in representations of some queens of the Middle Kingdom, shown as male, unlike the Greek sphinx which was female. Also, the Egyptian sphinx was viewed as benevolent, a guardian, whereas the Greek sphinx was invariably malevolent towards people. The sphinx was the embodiment of royal power."

83. For example, Alberto Siliotti, *Guide to the Pyramids of Egypt*, preface by Zahi Hawass; Farid Atiya, *The Giza Pyramids*; Verner, *op. cit.*

84. This view is reflected by Rainer Stadelmann in 'Royal Tombs from

the Age of the Pyramids', in *Egypt: The World of the Pharaohs*, p.75.

85. Reported to me by an Egyptologist who accompanied me to the Giza Pyramids in 2005; hinted at in several books.

86. See note 58.

87. See note 58.

88. Semti-Hesep-ti is referred to in Budge's 1899 edition of *The Book of the Dead*, p.210, as reigning "c.4266BC". This 1st-dynasty dating is clearly very wrong. Semti is missing from many lists of 1st-dynasty Pharaohs.

89. Lehner, "The Sphinx", in Zahi Hawass and others, *The Treasures of the Pyramids*, pp.179, 184; Lehner, *op. cit.*, p.132; Verner, *op. cit.*, p.237.

90. Lehner in Hawass, *op. cit.*, p.180: "The Sphinx must have been a repellent to dangerous forces."

91. Erik Iverson, *Obelisks in Exile*, vol 1, quoting Pliny's *Natural History*, 36. 14. 64.

92. For *sekhem*, see Budge, *The Book of the Dead (Theban Recension)*, p.lxii.

Index

Liberalis is a Latin word which evokes ideas of freedom, liberality, generosity of spirit, dignity, honour, books, the liberal arts education tradition and the work of the Greek grammarian and storyteller Antoninus Liberalis. We seek to combine all these interlinked aspects in the books we publish.

We bring classical ways of thinking and learning in touch with traditional storytelling and the latest thinking in terms of educational research and pedagogy in an approach that combines the best of the old with the best of the new.

As classical education publishers, our books are designed to appeal to readers across the globe who are interested in expanding their minds in the quest of knowledge. We cater for primary, secondary and higher education markets, homeschoolers, parents and members of the general public who have a love of ongoing learning.

If you have a proposal that you think would be of interest to Liberalis, submit your inquiry in the first instance via the website: www.liberalisbooks.com.